Praise for *El Rinche*

A heart-pounding, powerful story about the undying spirit of the Plata family—and how they fight to defend their land from being stolen, even in death.

—Natalia Sylvester, author of Author of
Chasing The Sun & Everyone Knows You Go Home

Christopher Carmona has created an unforgettable Chicano Ninja Superhero whose exploits re-imagine the time a century ago. Read the first page, and then hold on for this unfolding epic's latest turn.

—John Phillip Santos, author of
Places Left Unfinished at the Time of Creation

Finally, a novel that readers can learn about an alternative to the official myths of Texas Rangers and land developers who have been wrongly venerated for too long.

—Trinidad Gonzales,
Co-founder of *Refusing To Forget*

The contributions of Mexicans and Mexican Americans on the border has long been overlooked. Carmona takes a katana and slices the veil and gives us more than just an account; Carmona gives us a much needed hero.

—Juan Ochoa,
author of *Mariguano*

EL RINCHE

Matanza

Vol. 3

Christopher Carmona
El Rinche: Matanza | Vol. 3

First published in 2025 by Jade Publishing
UNITED STATES OF AMERICA

www.jadepublishing.org
ISBN: 978-1-949299-39-7

Printed in the United States of America

Dedication

This book is dedicated to the victims of the Matanza of 1915 and their descendants. To all those that have been the victims of state-sponsored violence. That violence and its injustice never leaves us. We must never forget.

Acknowledgments

I wish to acknowledge the research of The Reusing To Forget Project www.refusingtoforget.org and the support of my family and friends in completing this work.

EL RINCHE

Matanza

Vol. 3

CHRISTOPHER CARMONA

CONTENT

1. I Won't Back Down

2. Something to Believe In

3. Crossroad Blues

4. Volver Volver

5. Family Tradition

6. Zombie

7. Mad Mad World

8. Personal Jesus

9. Beds Are Burning

10. Runaway Train

11. Day In The Life

12. Father and Son

13. Ashes of San Miguel

14. Nothing Man

15. Evil is Alive and Well

16. Gimme Shelter

17. I'm Not Okay [I Promise]

18. Restless Sinner

19. Wake Up!

20. Who'll Stop The Rain

21. Working Class Hero

22. War Pigs

23. Kryptonite

24. Smooth Criminal

25. Bullet With Butterfly Wings

26. Demons

27. Violent

28. Voodoo

29. Soul To Squeeze

30. Landslide

31. Under Pressure

32. Just Breathe

33. Sweet Child of Mine

34. Times Like These

35. Sabotage

36. Disarm

37. A Hard Rain's A-Gonna Fall

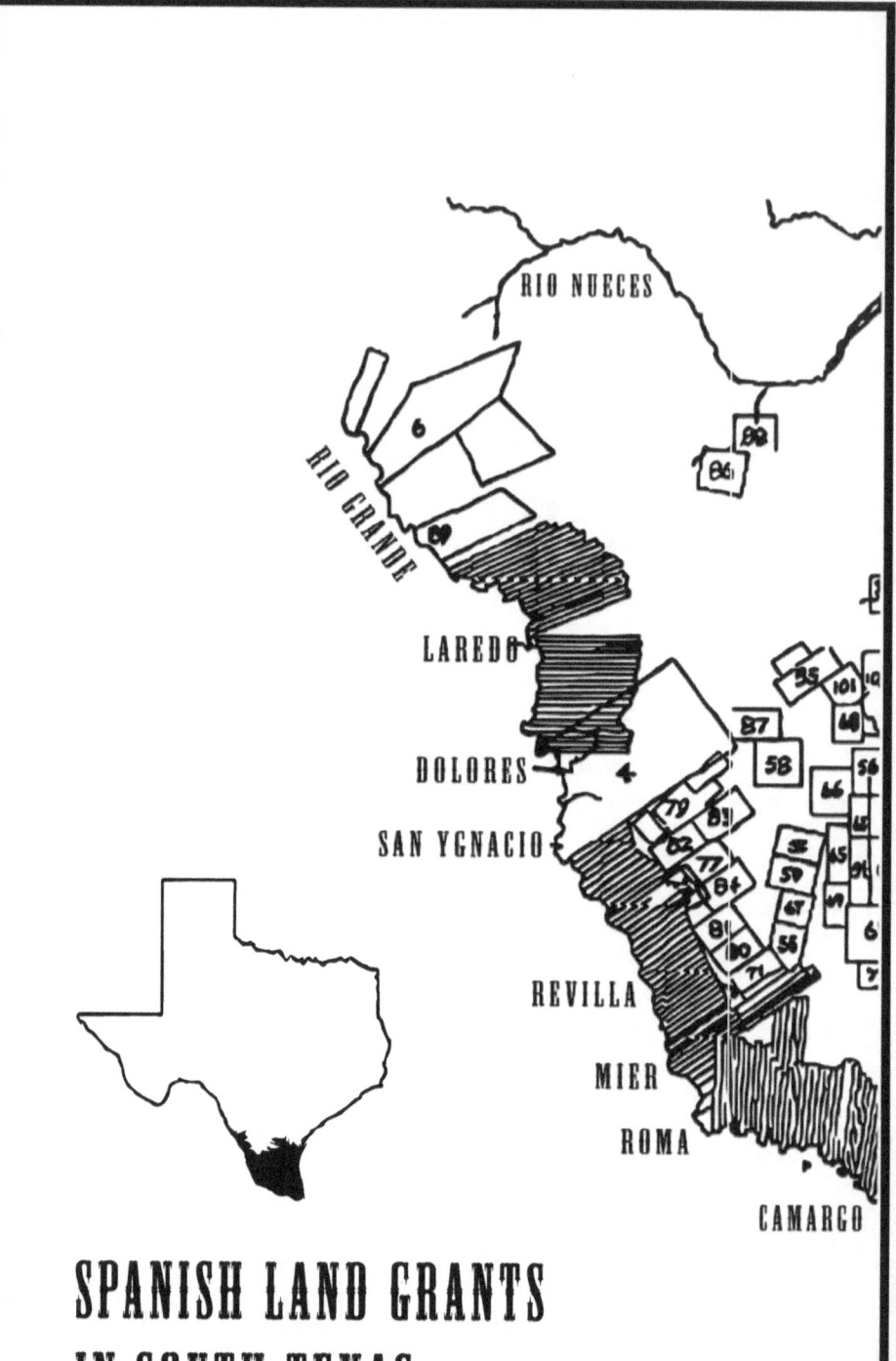

RIO NUECES

RIO GRANDE

LAREDO

DOLORES

SAN YGNACIO

REVILLA

MIER

ROMA

CAMARGO

SPANISH LAND GRANTS
IN SOUTH TEXAS

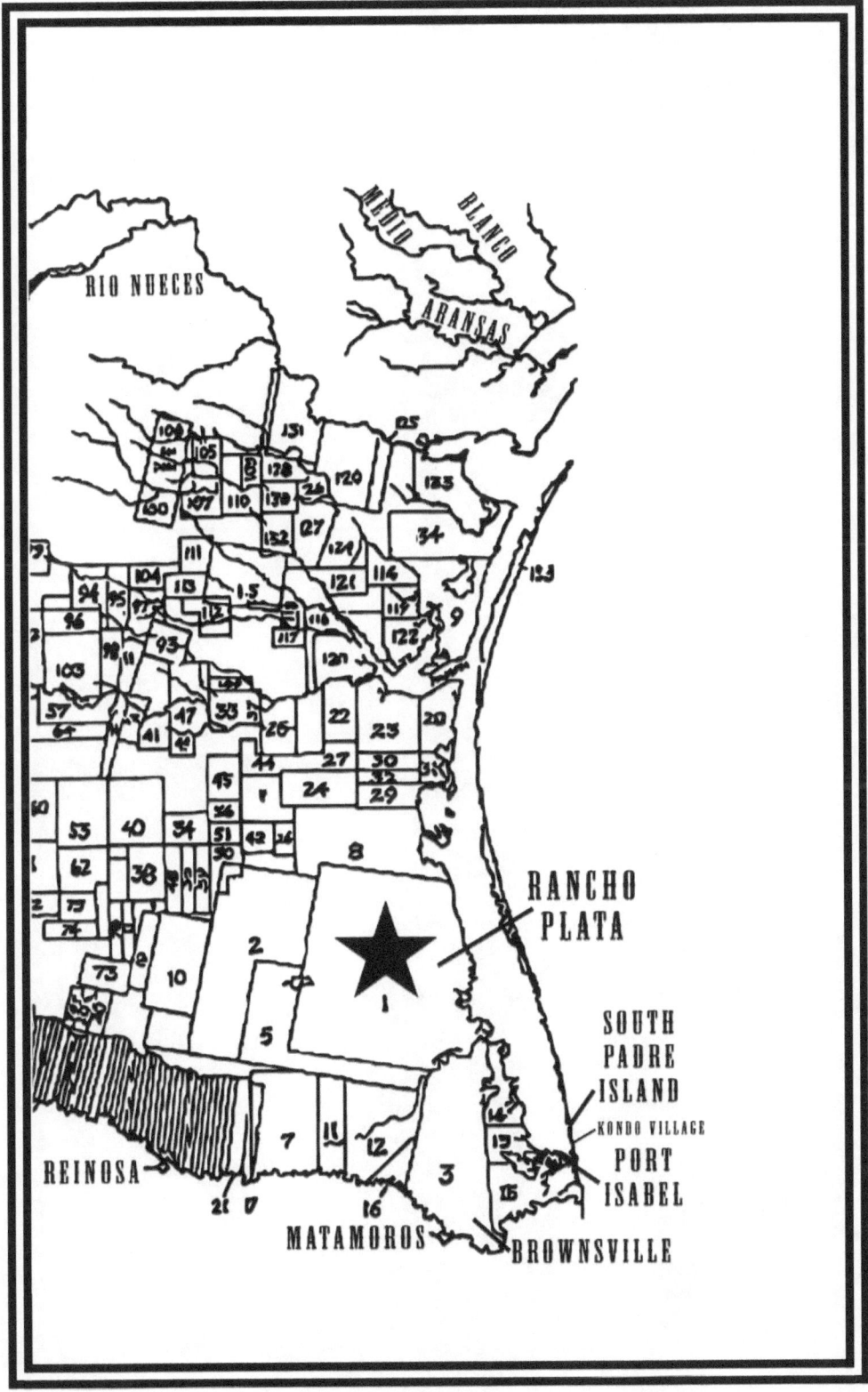

PART 1

I WON'T BACK DOWN

Well, I won't back down
No I won't back down
You could stand me up at the gates of Hell
But I won't back down

She stood behind her typesetter, Julio. The keys were cold. The paper loaded was an indictment on the Rinches. She had sworn she would never stop writing. Never stop telling the truth. Her fingers shook and her mind raced with fear, but she pulled the lever that would print the latest edition of El Progreso.

"Here we go," Jovita said as she pressed the paper and began to print the latest edition.

Her assistants, all men, smiled and began to get to work mass producing the day's newspaper with the headline: **President Woodrow Wilson's To Send United States Troops To The Border.** The article written under a pseudonym railed against using the violence on the border to bring troops. The executive order was written to stop the violence from the Mexican Revolution from spilling over, but Jovita knew better. It was to finalize the stealing of lands of Mexicano Tejanos for the Anglos. She did not relent in her accusations, and this was more than enough to call down the fury of the United States government on her little Laredo press. The word on the streets was clear. She must be stopped. The press must be stopped by any means necessary. Jovita had heard all of this, but she persisted.

"Señora!" Julio yelled, as he was looking out the window. "Los Rinches están aquí."

Jovita swallowed hard and looked up from her press. She straightened her skirts and walked outside. "Can I help you gentlemen?" Jovita said in her steadiest voice.

"You Idar?" the lead man in the white hat said butchering her name.

"Yes, I am Jovita Idár. What can I do for you?" she answered.

"My name is Captain Bob Rumsey. I am the head of the Texas Rangers here in Laredo and I am here to order you to seize and desist the printing of your press," the man said never getting off his horse.

Jovita looked up at him and said, "Captain, you know as well as I do that in this country our greatest right is the First. The right to the freedom of the press," she shot back.

"Señora, that only applies to Americans. Mexicans don't have no rights," Rumsey said with as much as confidence as any mediocre white man.

"Captain, I am an American and I will not stop printing my paper," Jovita shot back.

"You, señorita, are no American," Rumsey said feeling the anger rising.

"It astonishes me to find that so many of our countrymen should be contented to live under a system which leaves to their governors the power of taking from them the trial by jury in civil cases, freedom of religion, freedom of the press, freedom of commerce, the habeas corpus laws, and of yoking them with a standing army. This is a degeneracy in the principles of liberty… which I would not have expected for at least four centuries. Thomas Jefferson." Jovita recited from her recollections of the letters of Thomas Jefferson she had recently read.

"Who's that?" Rumsey said.

"You don't know your own founder of this here United States?" Jovita snarked.

"By the order of the governor of Texas and the President of the United States, you will stop printing, or face the consequences," Rumsey tried to change the subject.

"And what are those consequences?" Jovita said standing her ground.

"You know what they are. It's not a good time to be a Mexican in Texas," Rumsey said.

"Is that a threat from an officer of the law? Aren't you meant to uphold it?" Jovita said.

"Don't tell me my job. I follow orders and those orders are to stop this press," Rumsey said tiring of the conversation.

"Well, you shall not. Not today. Not as long as I am standing in your way," Jovita responded.

Rumsey was clearly furious at this Mexican woman talking to him with such conviction. "You will move, or I will make you move," was all he could muster.

"What are you going to do, Captain? Shoot me dead in the street in front of all of these witnesses. What do you think the rest of the papers will write when that happens?" Jovita said defiantly.

Rumsey just gripped the reins to his horse and simmered for a few seconds and then nodded to the other Rangers. Begrudgingly they turned and left.

Jovita felt like collapsing on the front steps of her press, but instead she turned and headed inside. This was a victory for sure.

There ain't no easy way out (I won't back down)
Hey I will stand my ground (I won't back down)
And I won't back down (I won't back down)
No I won't back down

SOMETHING TO BELIEVE IN

It wasn't so much the bullets that ripped through their bodies. It wasn't that they were left in a ditch on the side of the road. Carrion for the vultures to pick at. Not even the dogs would go near the scene. It wasn't any of those things that unsettled the winds today. It was the sound of click- click- click filling the dirt roads around the borderlands. That click- click- clicking sound sent a shiver down the spines of every Mexicano living in these lands. That sound that carried was white rage. White men with guns and badges. Brown lives never mattered, except to punctuate the ends of their bullets.

Jesús Bazan had known about all of this for the past couple of years. The cucarachas that the Rinches rode around in pierced the quiet ranch life of South Texas. They sent fear to everyone whose only crime was to be, but Jesús was a law-abiding man. A man of the people, a Hidalgo County commissioner. That would protect him, he believed. He needed to stay on the good side of the law. But on this night, he would learn that he might try to be on the good side of law, but the law was not ever on his side. He tried to stay neutral enough to be able to find resolutions for the many transgressions that the gente had been experiencing. This year in particular. The violence, the dead piling up, the stench of not being able to be buried. It was everywhere. Still, Jesús had to believe that right would prevail. That is why he reported the stealing of his horses by sediciosos from his corral.

He took his son-in-law Antonio Longoria along to report the theft. It was for the best, he told himself. He needed to get ahead of being accused of being a sympathizer. Which in these days meant meeting the wrath of the Rinches. So he decided to report.

The Ranger Captain, Henry Lee Ransom, and his men had set up camp on the Sam Lane Ranch. Jesús did not really trust Lane. He was always eyeing his lands, but never made a move to take it like so many others. Jesús believed his high esteem in the community would protect him. And so, on this night, Jesús and Antonio rode up on horseback to where a cucaracha was parked. Fresh mud tracks lead the two men to the three sitting on the porch of Lane's house.

"Evening Captain," Jesús said.

"Evening Señor Bazan, what can we do for you?" Ransom said with a bit of disdain in his voice.

"We just wanted to report that the sediciosos took some of my horses the other night. So, if you catch any of them and they have my brand, that's why," Jesús said humbly.

"When did this happen?" Ransom asked.

"About a couple of nights ago," Jesús responded.

"Why did you wait so long to report it?" Ransom asked

accusingly.

"Didn't know they were gone until today. My men just counted heads this morning," Jesús answered.

"Alright Señor Bazan, we will note that down and let you know if we come across them," Ransom said.

Jesús, feeling good about reporting the incident, thanked the Rinches, and he and Antonio turned and rode away.

Antonio had stayed quiet throughout the whole interaction, but when they were clear of the Lane Ranch turned to Jesús and said, "Do you think they are going to actually do anything about the horses?"

"No," Jesús answered, "but it needed to be done or else they will think we are helping the sediciosos."

"Do you really think they are that bad?" Antonio said.

"No, but these are precarious times Antonio, we have to play it smart if we are going to help la gente. I have to believe that our influence in this community can do some good," Jesús said trying to convince himself.

"I don't know. Things are so much worse now than they have ever been. I mean it has been so that any Mexicano can be shot down just for being Mexicano," Antonio said.

"I know, but we have to trust that justice will prevail."

"I don't know, it seems like white men are taking over and we don't know who we can trust," Antonio shot back.

"There are still a few good white men left," Jesús responded.

Then it came. The dreaded sound that every Mexicano feared. The click- click- clicking sound of a Ranger cucaracha.

25

It was dark out. The moon was barely peeking from behind the August clouds, but the headlights from the cucaracha shone bright from behind them.

"They must be on patrol tonight," Jesús said, "Let's get off the road and let them pass."

And so they did. They pulled their horses into the brush, and that's when it happened.

Oh, give me something to believe in (take the high road, give me something to believe in)
Oh, Lord arise (take the low road)
Give me something to believe in (take the high road, give me something to believe in)
Oh, Lord arise (take the low road)
Yeah, sometimes I wish to God I didn't know now
Things I didn't know then, yeah
And give me something to believe in

The ground welcomes us all in the end, Roland thought as he dug deep in the dirt. He didn't wear his gloves tonight. He didn't think it was appropriate. He had seen it all. The two men on horseback moving aside, the crappy cucaracha driving by real slow, the barrels of the guns, the flash of light. Then again, their intentions riddled the two men. The angels above wept, and Roland Warnock saw it all.

He had been working on the Bazan ranch all summer. He was a good man. He tried to help so much. He really believed that diplomacy was the way. That sticking by the law was the best option for protecting his people. Roland, being a white man himself, knew better. He never really trusted Sam Lane or the Rangers. He knew that they were up to no good. They didn't see ol' man Bazan as a man. They saw him as a Mexican. Roland had worked these South Texas ranches for years and he was always treated well by la gente. He liked them better than the Anglos here that was for sure. So, when he heard that the Rinches weren't letting ol' man Bazan and Antonio be buried he took it upon himself to help bury them. It was the least he could do.

It was such a quiet night that each strike of the shovel in the ground sounded so much louder than it should have. Roland wouldn't let that fear stop him from doing what was right. He was there with two other vaqueros. They were also good men, and if the Rinches saw them doing this, they would probably be shot. He might just be arrested because he was a white man, but he wasn't even sure of that.

Then it happened. He heard a fourth shovel digging in the ground. Roland looked up to see the Ghost Ranger dressed in full Ghost Ranger outfit, swords and all, digging with them. "I heard of you," Roland said to El Rinche.

"Don't believe everything you hear," El Rinche shot back.

"I don't, but you've been the talk of the town. A white man dressed up like a dead Rinche fighting for la gente," Roland said leaning on his shovel.

"Nowadays it seems that I'm doing a lot more burying than fighting. Didn't think they would take out Bazan," El Rinche said, saddened.

"Me either, but I saw it plain as day. Two rifles fired right at their back," Roland said.

"Who were they?" El Rinche asked.

"Didn't see their faces, but it don't take a genius to know that they were coming from the Lane Ranch. That there is Ransom's post," Roland said.

"Will you report that?" El Rinche asked.

"Already did. Ain't nothing gonna come of it, I don't think," Roland shot back as he flung the last clump of dirt over his shoulder.

"We can't lose hope. We have to have something to believe in or else all is lost," El Rinche said trying to convince himself.

"You sound like ol' man Bazan, but I don't know. Things seem to just be getting worse." Roland said. "I think it's deep enough now."

Roland, El Rinche, and the vaqueros slowly lowered the men into the ground and covered them back up. Behind him Roland heard the crunch of footsteps and turned to see a group of women with candles lit and veils coming up behind them. Roland turned to El Rinche to say something, but he was gone.

Uh, give me something to believe in (Uh, give me something to believe in)
If there's a Lord above
Uh, give me something to believe in, yeah (Uh, give me something to believe in)

MATANZA

Oh, Lord arise
Sometimes I wish to God I didn't know now
Things I didn't know then
Road you gotta take me home

EL RINCHE

CROSSROAD BLUES

Todd Mayfair had a bad run of luck in Houston. He had his truck jacked by a preacher who stole his shoes and his cargo. Now he was walking back to Houston in worn out preacher shoes. He could only remember what Mr. Guthrie had told him, "Don't let me down." And here he had gone and done that. He couldn't go back now, but he had nowhere else to go. So, he walked and walked until it got dark, and he couldn't see which way was up. Then like a light from heaven there was a crossroads lit by a single lamppost. The crossroads had a sign with two directions. One way headed to Houston. The other headed South. Todd scratched his head.

"Penny for your troubles," a deep voice came from out of the blue.

Todd jumped a little and said, "Geez, mister. You scared the hell out of me."

"Didn't mean to scare you, young man," the deep voice said stepping out of the shadow and revealing a black man in a pinstripe suit and a matching fedora. His eyes were darker than an abyss and he carried with him a guitar. He began to pluck at the strings.

"I bet you wondering what a snappy gent like me is doing out here in the middle of nowhere. Well, I tell you, I'm here to help you, little Todd Mayfair," the dark man said with a smile.

Todd, more than a little disturbed, said, "How'd you know me, my man?"

"I know a lot about you. But your name, oh well, that's the least I know about you," the dark man said.

"You talk awful uppity for a darkie," Todd shot back at him, "but you ain't answered my question."

"No need to be nasty little Todd. I'm here to help you," the dark man shot back.

"I don't need your help and please, stop calling me little Todd, only my…"

"Your grandma called you that," the dark man said cutting him off.

"Yeah, how'd you know that?" Todd said feeling very uneasy about his whole interaction.

"I told you Todd, I know all about you, and I am here to help you. You see, I only come when called and you called," the dark man said.

"I ain't called no one," Todd shot back.

"Oh yes, you did. You see, you at a crossroads and the decision you make tonight is going to shape the rest of your life. Be it great or not," the dark man said as he began to play a song.

I went to the crossroad, fell down on my knees
I went to the crossroad, fell down on my knees
Asked the Lord above, "Have mercy, now, save poor Todd if
you please"

As soon as Todd heard the song being strummed out on the guitar, he knew that he had called.

"What is that? That song?" Todd said with a sinking feeling in his throat.

"That is you," the dark man answered.

"Who are you?" Todd asked.

"Oh, I have many names, but tonight you can call me Ol' Scratch," the dark man said smiling.

"What? What is going on here?" Todd said with a tremor in his voice.

"Tonight, I am here to offer you a deal that will change you for the rest of your life. I will give you what you want most. Grit, ruthlessness, and power. The kind of power only a badge and a gun can give you," Ol' Scratch said still strumming his guitar.

"And what do you want in exchange?" Todd asked cautiously.

"The one thing you ain't using anyway, your soul." Ol' Scratch said.

"You the devil, ain't you? I heard about deals like this. It didn't end well for Faust," Todd said.

"You know Faust?" Ol' Scratch said.

"I been to school. We read Shakespeare," Todd responded.

"But didn't ol' Faust get exactly what he asked for?" Ol' Scratch said.

"Yeah. Yeah, he did," Todd said thinking about the offer, "How you gonna do that for me anyway?"

"Simple, we shake hands and make it a done deal and a car will come down this road and take you to your future with all the power you want," Ol' Scratch said as he stopped strumming.

Todd looked down at the raggedy Preacher shoes and then back at Ol' Scratch and then he stuck his hand out. "Worth a shot. Besides I don't believe in no souls anyway."

Ol' Scratch laughed a deep laugh and caught Todd's hand. Todd felt a sharp prick in his palm and pulled his hand back. "Deals like this can only be signed in blood," Ol' Scratch said as drifted into the darkness.

Todd stood there alone for a minute and thought he had been duped by some darkie on the side of the road. But then he heard the click- click- clicking of a motorcar. Then lights over the horizon and Todd smiled knowing that this was his ride.

And I went to the crossroad, mama, I looked East and West
I went to the crossroad, baby, I looked East and West

Naomi washed her hands after a long shift selling shrimp at the market when she told Itsuko that she would meet her back at the village later. She had a date with a man she wasn't sure of. Mostly because he was a white man. But a white man with a good heart. He was also a preacher.

"Naomi," called a voice from behind her.

Naomi smiled and turned to see her date, Jacob Freeman. "Jacob, you're early. I was just cleaning up."

"No worries. I was just picking stuff up for the church. Lord knows that refugees are nothing if not starving," Jacob said smiling.

Naomi walked into his arms, and they embraced with a kiss.

Jacob caught his reflection in a window and saw a face he had not seen in years. A man he was in the past. A long straggly bearded scoundrel. Jacob blinked and there he was as he was now. A clean-cut preacher.

"What's wrong, Jacob?" Naomi said noticing a change in his demeanor.

"Nothing," Jacob said snapping himself out of it, "Just thought I saw someone I used to know. Let's go."

Jacob put his arm around her shoulder, and they began to walk off when Jacob heard the familiar strumming of guitar strings. That song sent a shiver down his spine. *"Standin' at the crossroad, baby, risin' sun goin' down. I believe to my soul, now, poor Pablo, is sinkin' down…"* Jacob felt the song leaving his lips before he even realized it.

"What's that you singing?" Naomi asked.

"An old song I heard on the road once a long time ago."

VOLVER VOLVER

Tiburcio Treviño waited all day to have a few drinks at the Sunshine Bar and see los otros vaqueros. They worked hard every day, and this was their only comfort. He rode his horse deep into town where the bar stood. The streets were not like they were just two weeks ago. The pavement covered many of the roads and los carros were starting to clutter the city. The noise and the smoke were too much for Tiburcio, but he couldn't do much about it. He was lucky to still have his job, the rancho business was drying up. Trains and farms were now taking over. This, amongst other reasons, was why Tiburcio was drinking tonight.

He pulled his horse to the front of the bar and tied his trusty Chivo to the post. He was called Chivo because he was always stubborn in the mornings. He walked inside to hear the local músico strumming away on his guitar. He sang: *Este amor apasionado. Anda todo alborotado. Por Volver. Voy camino a la locura y aunque todo me tortura. Sé querer. Nos dejamos hace tiempo. Pero me llegó el momento. De perder. Tú tenías mucha razón. Le hago caso al corazón. Y me muero por Volver.*

Tiburcio strode up to the bar and order una cerverza and turned to see the crowd that was forming in the barroom. Vaqueros and damas talking and drinking together. It was heaven for Tiburcio. He was on the hunt for a woman to settle down with and have a few kids, but he had no such luck in his twenty-three years. Most of the other vaqueros already had a wife and kids. He felt he was behind the curb and so tonight he swore he would find someone. The bartender slid an open beer bottle to him, Tiburcio picked it up and took a long swig.

He took to drinking and talking with some of the other vaqueros and danced a few bailes with the local barmaids. The music picked up with the addition of an accordion and a bass guitar. Then he saw her. She sat by herself at the bar. Long dark hair. Her face not quite Mexicana, maybe a bit more something else. She was dressed in men's clothes. Pants and boots he was not familiar with. A vest made of purple and white beads and a red kerchief around her neck. The woman turned and looked at him and he smiled. She quickly turned away, but that didn't deter Tiburcio. He simply strode over to her and said, "¿cómo está señorita?"

The woman didn't even look at him when she said, "You're barking up the wrong tree güey. Move on."

Tiburcio didn't speak English too well, but he understood a brush off in any language. Before he could respond, the room went quiet as three Texas Rangers walked through the front door. Tiburcio turned to look at these gringos in their white hats and tiny badges. He then turned back to the woman to say something, but she was gone.

"Alright, listen up here. My name is Todd Mayfair and I'm here looking for a man by the name of Benicio Plata," said the tall skinny Rinche who looked too young to be a Rinche.

"No hay nadie aqui con ese nombre," said the head bartender.

"Is that right?" said Todd as he touched his gun. "Then how about Ti-bur-c-i-o Ramos?"

Tiburcio swallowed hard because he almost thought they called his name. The other vaqueros started whispering to each other and giving side-long glances at Tiburcio. He didn't know what to do, so he took another drink from his beer.

"Well, well, well…" Todd said, "looks like everyone's talking about you, chico."

Tiburcio knew that the tall, skinny Rinche was looking at him. The other Rangers turned in his direction. Tiburcio looked around, but no one was looking at him. "Yo no soy Tiburico Ramos," Tiburcio said feeling the fear creeping up like a slow-moving snake.

"Then what's your name, chico?" Todd said sliding his gun from his holster.

"Ni nombre es Tiburcio…"

"…I thought you said your wasn't Tybur c..e..o," Todd said cutting him off.

"Sí pero…" was all Tiburcio could get out before Todd stuck the gun in his face and cocked the hammer.

Tiburcio closed his eyes expecting his life to end at that moment, but then a miracle happened.

"He's not the one you are looking for," came a forceful female voice with a bit of a Japanese accent.

Todd pulled the gun from Tiburcio's face and turned to see a woman dressed in a beaded vest and a red kerchief over her face and two sticks in her hands.

"And what are you supposed to be, little lady?" Todd said.

"I'm a reckoning," the masked woman said.

The other Rinches already had their guns trained on the woman and Todd pointed his at her and said, "It ain't too smart bringing sticks to a gun fight."

"These are special," the woman said raising the stick to the Rinche on her left and said, "Bang."

Todd was just about to laugh when the gun exploded out of his partner's hand. Then the woman pointed the other stick at the rinche to her left and said, "Bang."

Once again, the gun exploded in his hand, and he stumbled back gripping his hand in pain.

Todd was baffled by what just happened. Confused he said, "You one of them Ghost Rinches, ain't you?"

The woman moved so fast that Todd didn't even see how she got right in front of him. "How'd you do that?" he said dumbfounded.

"Magic," she responded as she knocked the gun from his hand and knocked him across the head. He fell to the floor like a sack of potatoes.

The woman looked around the room and saw the other two rinches frozen from confusion and fear, "The men you are looking for aren't here. Take your trash with you and get out."

The two rinches collected Todd and rushed out of the bar.

The woman looked around the room and said, "Sorry about that. They won't be back."

"But what if they do come back?" said the head bartender.

"Then tell them El Rinche is watching," the woman said as she walked out of the room.

Tiburcio swallowed hard. He was in love.

Junko exited the bar and started following the two rinches as they put their boss into their cucaracha. She stayed to the shadows and watched when a voice came from behind her, "That was exciting."

"It was stupid, but necessary Tal'dos," Junko said.

"Listen, I think we should talk," Tal'dos said as she was distracted with the rinches.

"Not now, these three are up to no good and things are getting really bad out there. What the hell have you all been doing since I've been gone?" Junko said sounding a little annoyed.

"We've been doing what we can, but we can't be everywhere and now they are talking about bringing in the military," Tal'dos said.

"And what about Bennie? Have you found him yet?" Junko asked.

"Well, finding him isn't the problem. It's getting him to come home. Like someone I know," Tal'dos said.

Junko turned to look at him and then turned back to

watching the rinches. "Look, I can't go back. Not yet."

"You still mad at Hiro and your mother?" Tal'dos asked knowing the answer.

"They lied to me. So, no I don't think I'm ready to move back home," Junko said. "They're leaving. I'm gonna follow. Are you coming with me?"

Tal'dos sighed and said, "Of course. Volver, Volver is never as good as it sounds."

Y volver volver, volver
A tus brazos otra vez
Llegaré hasta donde estés
Yo sé perder, yo sé perder
Quiero volver, volver volver

FAMILY TRADITION

Inez awoke with a start. She felt the waves of nausea coming over her. She barely made it to the bucket at the end of her bedroom. "Oh God," Inez said after she finished hurling up last night's dinner, "not again."

"Are you okay?" Chonnie said rising from the bed.

"Yeah, it's just last night's mole didn't agree with me," Inez lied.

"Junko and Tal'dos are supposed to be heading to Kondo today. Junko's finally gonna talk to her mother," Chonnie said stretching and pouring Inez a glass of water.

Chonnie walked over and handed her the water. "Thanks," she said with a forced smile, "but I can't keep anything down right now."

"Are you sure it isn't something more serious?" Chonnie said caressing her face.

Inez looked at him and got to her feet. "No, it will pass. I am sure. Listen, I have to get the day started. There are cattle to attend to," she said with a coldness in her voice.

Chonnie knew that tone. She was angry and it was probably something he did that he couldn't quite understand. He would ask Tal'dos later. "Okay, I guess I'll head back to Kondo."

"Why don't you try and find my son today?" Inez shot at him as she walked out of the room, slamming the door behind her.

Chonnie stood there knowing there was nothing he could say to her. When it came to Bennie, Chonnie learned to say nothing. It was best to let the anger pass. Chonnie knew exactly where Bennie was, but it wasn't quite so easy getting to him. He was with Aniceto and the other sediciosos. Aniceto swore he would keep Bennie safe, but Chonnie wasn't so sure. He was right in the middle of a brewing war. Aniceto had become so cold and rageful after the death of his daughter. That was what brought Bennie closer to Aniceto, their shared grief over Serafina. But Bennie didn't blame the Grandmaster who was actually behind her death. Instead, he blamed El Rinche, and Aniceto thought it was best they keep their distance. The worst part of the whole nasty situation was that he wouldn't even talk to his mother. It was driving Inez crazy.

Chonnie got dressed and then stepped into the shadows. Gone like the night.

Inez stood outside the bedroom door. The tears slowly traveling their crooked road down her face.

"Señora, are you alright?" said Señora García, Inez's most trusted caretaker.

Inez wiped the tears from her face and said, "Sí, señora García. I am fine. Did you need something?"

"¡Está embarazada!" Señora García said, as she touched

Inez's stomach.

Inez could never fool Señora García, and she broke down and started to sob.

"Ay mija. This is a good thing," Señora García said, hugging Inez.

"No, how am I going to explain this? I am not married. I am having the baby of a ghost," Inez sobbed.

"You haven't told Señor Chonnie?" Señora García asked, knowing the answer.

"I want to, but I don't know," Inez said, feeling the tears subsiding.

"We will figure this out, but you have to tell Señor Chonnie," Señora García said, handing Inez a handkerchief to wipe her tears.

"I know, but it seems like a family tradition not to," Inez said, sarcastically.

Junko and Tal'dos stood on the ferry to Kondo village with their horses, still dressed for superheroing. Junko had her eyes closed breathing in the salt air. It was a smell she had missed while chasing her father and his hornets across the dusty borderlands of New Mexico. And when she found him, it did not go as planned.

"It's a beautiful morning," Tal'dos said trying to break the silence.

"I guess you Indians don't know the importance of silence," Junko snapped at Tal'dos.

"Sorry, I was just trying…"

"...No, I'm sorry. I'm just feeling anxious. We don't exactly talk about our feelings in our family. It's our family's greatest tradition," Junko said.

"I'm here. No matter what," Tal'dos said trying to be reassuring.

"I know, I know. But sometimes, I got to handle these things on my own," Junko said.

The ferry began to shake, interrupting their conversation, signaling it was about to make landfall. Tal'dos and Junko untied their horses and began to make their way off the ferry when they heard a familiar voice.

"There's my favorite niece and my favorite Indian," Hiro said trying to smile.

"Uncle Hiro, it's good to see you," Junko said as she hugged him. "I'm still mad at you and mamá, but it is good to see you nonetheless."

"Junko, I have missed you," Itsuko's voice came from behind Hiro.

Junko just glared at her and said, "Let's get back to the hideout. We have a lot to talk about." Junko looked around and asked, "Where's Mayako?"

Itsuko answered, "She's late as usual. You know your sister."

Lateness. Another family tradition.

The gang headed back to their hideout and Itsuko began to make tea.

"Where's Naomi? I assumed she would be glued to your hip," Junko said sending a barb at her mother.

"She's handling the shop today, so that we could talk," Itsuko said trying not to strike out at her daughter for such disrespect. She kept it inside for the sake of their relationship.

After the tea was hot, they began to sip it in tense silence until finally Junko broke, "Why didn't you tell me that my father was still alive?"

And there it was. No pretense like Japanese tradition called for. Being in America had certainly had its effect on her daughter, Itsuko thought.

"Your father is dead. The man you think is your father is something else entirely," Hiro said.

"Really, because he seemed pretty alive when I spoke with him. He looks like my father. He remembers when Mayako and me were small. He even remembers when you left him for dead in the battle of Toba–Fushimi. He told me everything," Junko said letting all of resentment spill out.

"There is much you don't know about your father and what happened at Toba-Fushimi," Itsuko said trying not to fall apart.

"Atoy betrayed us all. He sold us out for a few dollars and a promise that your mother and you and your sister would be safe," Hiro said.

"That's not what he says. He says you betrayed him. You left him to die," Junko shot back.

"Listen to me, Junko. I don't know who that man is that you have been talking to, but your father is dead. I saw him die," Hiro said.

"He said you would say that, so he told me to tell you that

Hattori Hanzō is coming," Junko said.

Hiro's eyes widened and said, "Did he say when?"

Junko confused said, "No, he just said to tell you that. Why is Hattori Hanzō, a ninja mythical figure coming? He's supposed to be long dead."

"The Demon King," Itsuko said with fear gripping her. "He's coming to claim his due."

Hiro looked at Itsuko, who was clearly shaken, and said, "I won't let that happen. Not as long as I am alive."

Junko confused asked, "What's going on?"

Itsuko walked over to her daughter and grabbed both of her arms and said, "That man that says he is your father, is not. There is terrible evil coming."

"You got that right," Mayako said walking in with Jovita in tow, "They burned down El Progreso and the sediciosos are about to stir up a hornet's nest."

Everyone just looked at Mayako not knowing what to say. Mayako saw Junko and said, "Oh, hey, Junko. Welcome home."

"Trouble. That's also a family tradition, isn't it?" Junko said.

"Always," Mayako answered.

ZOMBIE

Another head hangs lowly
Child is slowly taken
And the violence caused such silence
Who are we mistaken?

It had been a long time coming, Frank Hamer told himself as he puffed on his cigar. Here he was. On his way back into the fold. Fox, the Captain of the Rangers in South Texas, needed his brand of justice, and Frank was more than happy to comply. He had been working a dead-end job as a cattle thief investigator in Kimble County. He was definitely bored and itching to get into real work. Fox caught up with him in Houston and offered him a deal he couldn't refuse.

"Pancho, things are bad on the border right now," Fox said calling him by his nickname. "The Mexicans aren't complying like they should be. This Rinche character is giving them too much hope."

"You need the Mexicans in their place, or you need the

Mexicans gone? Because the first is already difficult with the law and the second is going to need reassurances," Hamer said as he took a swig of Fox's expensive whiskey. They sat in Houston's new and upcoming social bar, the Golden Nugget. It was run by the famous Indian marshal, Grant Johnson. It was the place to be for the top brass of law enforcement. Johnson even worked the bar himself and he would charge people one dollar to take a photograph with him. It was a racket, and all the top law dogs loved it.

"We need the Mexicans compliant, whatever means necessary and…" Fox said putting a Texas Ranger badge in front of him. "This time, though, the Governor, he's got your back."

"No prosecution?" Hamer said more than a little amused.

"We are the special Rangers. We only answer to the Governor," Fox said downing the rest of his whiskey.

"If I do this, Jimmie, you gotta know that it ain't going to be pretty," Hamer said.

"I know. That's why I came to you," Fox said smiling.

Hamer reached over the table and shook Fox's hand and then grabbed the badge, "When do I start?" Hamer asked.

"Right away."

Hamer was interrupted with his trip down memory lane when his driver said, "Boss?"

"Yeah, Scott," Hamer shouted to his driver.

"There's a kid in the road," Scott said, looking at Hamer through the rearview mirror.

"What? What kid?" Hamer said confused about why he

should care.

"He's flagging us down," Scott said, not knowing what to do.

Hamer, now curious, looked out his side window and saw this skinny kid with worn out shoes waving him down. Hamer felt the need to stop and help this kid. He didn't know why but he felt he knew him. "Pull over, Scott."

Scott pulled the car over and Hamer rolled down his window. "Hey kid, what are you doing out here in the middle of nowhere?"

The kid walked up to his window and said, "Are you the man I'm supposed to see?"

"The crossroads man send you?" Hamer said.

"Yes, sir," the kid said with a big tooth grin.

"Then get in," Hamer said opening the door for the kid.

The kid got in and the cucaracha started on its way again. "My name is Todd Mayfair. I'm ready for my new life."

"Frank Hamer, Texas Ranger. Is that what the ol' man said to you?" Hamer said.

"He said you was my future," Todd said.

Hamer sized the kid up and said, "Why do you think ol' Scratch sent you to me?"

Todd looked at Hamer and said, "Mister, he said you could give me power like I never had before."

Hamer smiled and liked this kid immediately, "We are heading to the border to take care of some bandidos. They ain't been complying. We got to do what needs to be done. Are you up for that? Any means necessary?"

Todd looked him dead in the eye and said, "Mister, any means necessary is what I've been waiting for my entire life. Especially if it is about killing Mexicans and darkies."

"Oh yeah, you don't like Mexicans and Blacks?" Hamer said liking this kid even more.

"Sir, this here is the white man's land. It's about time that the darker species of this earth realize that the white man is the ultimate man," Todd said smiling.

"Yes, son. That is what I am talking about. But it's not just this land here. It's the world that belongs to the white man. Take this here what's happening in Haiti. These niggers just assassinated their own president. And why? Because they didn't want to deal with the United States. And so, they took out their own leader, like savages. But President Wilson, he wasn't having any black rebels stop our interests, so he invaded Haiti. We now occupy them like we should," Hamer said finally finding a captive audience for his world views.

"I read about that. Isn't that where all those zombie stories come from?" Todd asked.

"They're all zombies. Running around thinking they're not, but they are. Mindless. Only good for working the fields, working for us. They ain't people. No, not like us," Hamer said.

"But isn't there this Garvey fella stirring up the darkies to fight against the white man? He was in Houston not too long ago," Todd said.

"Garvey is an ape with his rights for blacks talk. He ain't

never going to be nothing. The white man always wins. Like in Haiti, and like we are going to do in South Texas," Hamer said looking at the passing trees.

South Texas, Todd thought, *that's where that devious preacher was heading. This is truly the right path.*

> *But you see, it's not me*
> *It's not my family*
> *In your head, in your head, they are fighting*
> *With their tanks and their bombs*
> *And their bombs and their guns*
> *In your head, in your head, they are crying…*

MAD MAD WORLD

And I find it kinda funny
I find it kinda sad
The dreams in which I'm dying
Are the best I've ever had
I find it hard to tell you
I find it hard to take
When people run in circles
It's a very, very mad world, mad world...

"You know, I have these dreams where we aren't losing. Where kids can be free to play outside without rinches coming for their fathers. I have these dreams and I hate them because all I see around us is this," Jovita said pointing to the burnt down remnants of her newspaper offices.

"Jovita, we still have the Brownsville office," Mayako assured her.

"I don't think I can do this anymore," Jovita said feeling hopeless.

"Hey," Mayako said grabbing Jovita by the shoulders, "look at me."

Jovita raised her eyes and looked at Mayako.

"We can't give up. We still have a working press and if we don't get back and protect that one, then they will have won. I won't give up, and I won't leave you. Now, wipe those tears off your face, and get your ass on that train. We are heading back to the Rinche cave," Mayako said with grit.

Jovita felt herself coming back, she nodded.

"They destroyed everything," Mayako recounted to the gang. "Where's Chonnie anyway?"

"Right here," Chonnie said coming in through the door of their hideout on Kondo Village. "What's going on?"

"Things are worse than ever. Los Rinches burned down Jovita's press in Laredo and they are going to be coming for us here next. I know it," Mayako said with a fire she had never felt.

"We know," Chonnie said sounding defeated.

"There is something brewing from the sediciosos. They are building an army and I fear that the killings will only get worse," Tal'dos said.

"What are we going to do?" Mayako asked.

"I am going to meet Aniceto. I will find out what is going on," Chonnie said.

Junko, who had stayed quiet contemplating her past and her mother's lies, knew she needed to focus that energy back into the cause and said, "I will go with you."

"Thank you, Junko, but Aniceto is just expecting me," Chonnie said.

"Oh, they won't see me. I just need to do a little spy work," Junko said smiling.

"The army is on its way, and when that happens, nothing good ever comes," Tal'dos added.

"This is such a mad world. We fight and we fight, and yet it's like two steps forward and one step back. The violence just brings on more violence. Can't we just take them out where it counts?" Jovita pleaded.

"What do you have in mind?" Tal'dos asked.

"We target them politically," Jovita said feeling her fire coming back.

"What are we doing here, son?" Macario whispered to Bennie.

Bennie had been running with the sediciosos since Serafina died and Aniceto took him in. He had only been a gopher and never been able to be a real revolutionary. It had been three years and he had been on the run the entire time. Learning to shoot, track, fight. It was everything that he wanted to be. The whole time, his father Macario, had been by his side. His father had found him when he was at his lowest point. He had picked him up and told him who the true enemy was, El Rinche. But his mother…

"She is fine. She needs you to be a man now," Macario said, distracting him from his thoughts.

"I just would like to see her again," Bennie said, out loud.

"I know, I know. But our work is not done yet. You must focus on the cause and getting to El Rinche, he let Serafina die," Macario whispered in his ear again.

"El Rinche, the hero of the people. My ass. This war, that is the way," Bennie said seething with anger.

"That's the spirit. Don't forget, you are a sedicioso now. You are going to win this for our people," Macario said, filled with excitement.

"He will not survive this meeting with Aniceto. I will make sure of it," Bennie said under his breath.

"Bennie, are you ready?" Aniceto called to Bennie.

Bennie turned to see Aniceto and Luis del Rey mounting their horses. "I'm ready."

"Bennie, there has been a change of plans," Aniceto said.

"What's that?" Bennie asked.

"You're not coming with us today," Aniceto said knowing that it would upset Bennie.

"What? Why not?" Bennie said, angrily.

"We need you to do something else," Luis broke the tension between the two of them.

Aniceto jumped back in and said, "We need you to be Basilio Ramos and take the plan to McAllen."

"What? Now? Isn't it a little too early for that?" Bennie protested.

"No, the Rangers burned down Jovita's press, we need to step things up. We need the U.S. military to come here, and the plan is the only way," Luis explained.

"I really wanted to go to this meeting tonight," Bennie simmered.

"I know, but I don't think that is a good idea," Aniceto jumped back in.

"Why is that?" Bennie's anger was seeping through his words.

"You know why, Bennie. You're too hot," Aniceto said.

"He's not a friend to the cause, he let Serafina die," Bennie was furious.

"That's not what happened. I know, I was there," Aniceto shot back at Bennie feeling his own anger rising.

"Don't listen to him. El Rinche must die," Macario whispered in Bennie's ear.

"Listen Bennie, we need you to do this. Head to McAllen tonight. Be Basilio. The cause is what matters most. It is what she would have wanted," Luis jumped in once again calming down the tension.

Bennie looked at Luis and felt the anger subside. "Okay, I will get ready. But his day will come."

All around me are familiar faces. Worn out places, worn out faces. Bright and early for their daily races. Going nowhere, going nowhere. Their tears are filling up their glasses. No expression, no expression. Hide my head, I wanna drown my sorrow. No tomorrow, no tomorrow," Macario sang softly. Only Bennie could hear it.

"And I find it kinda funny I find it kinda sad. The dreams in which I'm dying. Are the best I've ever had. I find it hard to tell you. I find it hard to take. When people run in circles. It's a very, very mad world, mad world," Bennie sang out loud.

59

EL RINCHE

PERSONAL JESUS

Your own personal Jesus
Someone to hear your prayers
Someone who cares
Your own personal Jesus
Someone to hear your prayers
Someone who's there…

Jacob couldn't believe he could ever be happy. He watched as the moonlight bounced off Naomi's skin. So soft. He couldn't believe any of this. He had only been Jacob for three years. And his luck was always on the edge of failing him. It was quite an ordeal becoming Jacob Freeman. He had to lose himself. His old self. And be reborn a new man. But like any rebirth, it was not without death and pain and loss on a scale he would never be able to tell anyone about. Not even Naomi. The love of his life.

"Whatcha doing?" Naomi asked awaking from a slumber.

"Nothing, just admiring you," Jacob said as he brought her in for a hug.

"Ohhh, that's sweet," Naomi responded half-asleep.

"You know when I look at you, two words come to mind," Jacob spoke softly into her ear.

"Yeah, what are they?" Naomi asked playing along.

"The first is Yakamoz. It's Turkish. It means the reflection of the moonlight on water."

"And the second," Naomi said smiling just a little.

"The second is Yugen. It's Japanese. It means a profound, mysterious sense of the beauty of the universe … and the sad beauty of human suffering." Jacob didn't know if he meant her, or the life he now lived.

"That's beautiful. Thank you," Naomi said turning over to give Jacob a kiss.

Jacob met her kiss with passion and then in a flash of time he was transported back to that day when he became Jacob. He was walking along a dusty backroad when a crazy kid picked him up. The kid spewed his racist crap, and for the first time in his life, Jacob did the right thing. It was because of that kid that led him to his path of redemption.

"But that wasn't the end of it, was it?" came a dark voice that Jacob recognized oh so well.

"No, it wasn't," Jacob said in this dream.

"What happened next, Man Who Lost His Name?" the voice teased him.

"We drove and drove and then," Jacob stumbled, "and then…"

"And then you came to a crossroads," the voice said.

"Yes, I came to a crossroads. I stopped the truck and looked all four ways, but couldn't for the life of me figure out which way to go. Until…" Jacob said in a trancelike state.

"Until Ol' Scratch came along," the voice said relishing this conversation.

"Yes, until you came along," Jacob said feeling his heart sinking in his chest.

"And then you made a deal," Ol' Scratch laughed.

"Yes…no…" Jacob said trying to shake off this dream.

He closed his eyes and he felt hot winds on his back. When he opened them, he saw himself in Brownsville. In front of a run-down building. Justicio, Leticia, and their son, Rodrigo smiled at him as they started to take everything down from the truck. Jacob got off the truck and saw what was to be his church.

"Padre, how do you like it?" Rodrigo asked.

"It's perfect, Rodrigo," Jacob said still in his trance.

Rodrigo began to strum his guitar and then began to sing, *"Feeling unknown. And you're all alone. Flesh and bone. By the telephone. Lift up the receiver. I'll make you a believer…"*

Jacob looked at Rodrigo and said, "Reach out, touch faith."

"That's it. Remember," Ol' Scratch whispered in Jacob's ear.

"I know all this. Why do you want me to remember this?" Jacob said angrily.

"Because this ain't who you are, is it?" Ol' Scratch answered.

"This is who I am. This is who I chose to be," Jacob said trying to convince himself.

"Is it? Or is because of the deal you made, Man Who Lost

His Name?" Ol' Scratch said.

"What do you want from me?" Jacob shouted.

"What do you think we should name the church, Padre," Rodrigo asked strumming his guitar.

Jacob looked around and said, "We should call it Vida Nueva Baptist Church. Because that's what this is going to be for everyone who walks through those doors."

Rodrigo smiled and began singing again, *"Take second best. Put me to the test. Things on your chest. You need to confess. I will deliver. You know I'm a forgiver."*

"Reach out, touch faith. Reach out, touch faith," Jacob responded.

Jacob closed his eyes and felt the room spin. It was two months later, and the church was finished. The sign hung above the door, Vida Nueva Baptist Church. But still the only parishioners were the Guerra's and a couple of their friends. Jacob was writing his sermon in the back pew when a soft woman's voice interrupted him.

"Hello, are you Preacher Freeman?" Naomi said to Jacob. It was the first time they ever met.

"Yes, I am," Jacob responded and stood up to greet her.

"Ain't this a treat. A Baptist in Catholic country," Naomi said looking around.

"Yes, I know it's unusual, but the Baptist faith saved me, and I thought I would spread the Word," Jacob explained.

"Ain't much business though?" Naomi said looking around.

Jacob chuckled a little and said, "No, not yet. But I got

hope."

Naomi smiled at him and said, "Well, I might be able to help you with that."

Jacob was already smitten with this ebony beauty, but now she was going to help.

"I got a bunch of Black folk looking for a church of their own. You see, they are escaping the troubles in the ol' South and are settling here to make a new life for themselves. I didn't know what to tell them until I saw your sign: Nueva Vida. That was sign enough for me," Naomi said.

"I would be happy to have them here, but you know I'm not black," Jacob said sheepishly.

"I won't hold it against you," Naomi said smiling at him.

Jacob chuckled, "Well, okay then, see you all Sunday at 10 AM sharp."

"They'll be here," Naomi said turning to leave.

"And what about you? You're not coming?" Jacob said.

"I ain't the church type. I have my faith in other things," Naomi responded.

"One service. Sunday. That's all I ask and then you can decide if it's for you or not," Jacob plead with Naomi.

"Preacher, I don't know," Naomi said wavering.

"*Feeling unknown. And you're all alone. Flesh and bone. By the telephone. Lift up the receiver. I'll make you a believer. I will deliver. You know I'm a forgiver. Reach out, touch faith. Your own personal Jesus,*" Jacob sang to her.

"Is that from the bible?" Naomi asked.

"No, from a young boy who has the gift of music," Jacob answered.

"Okay. Okay. I will see you Sunday, but no promises," Naomi said walking out.

Jacob flashed back to the bedroom that he shared with Naomi. He was still holding her in his arms. She was fast asleep, but he wasn't. There was a dread rising in him and he swore he could hear them. The hellhounds were on his trail.

BEDS ARE BURNING

Mayako was no shadow-walker like Chonnie or her sister, but she knew how to stay hidden. It was a skill that she learned from being a woman reporter in a man's world. No one really paid attention to the little Asian woman with a pen and a pad. The Mexicans assumed she didn't speak Spanish. The Gringos assumed she didn't speak English. They were both wrong. And on this night, she needed to put her skills to the test against the best shadow-walkers she had ever known: the Rinche gang.

"You can't come," Junko said putting her foot down.

"Why not? This will be a great story," Mayako plead with Junko.

"Mayako, you know you can't print any of this. We are a secret superhero organization," Junko responded annoyed at her little sister.

"I know that. I would never reveal any information about the gang, but I need to help. This is huge. Jovita is going to see some politician. You are all going to meet with the sediciosos. What am I going to do?" Mayako said frustrated.

"Stay here with mamá and Uncle Hiro. They could use the company," Junko shot the jab at her mother.

Itsuko looked at Junko with a look of despair and hurt and said, "Listen to your sister, Mayako. She knows what's best. I don't want you to get hurt."

Hiro stayed quiet the whole time. He had a plan, but he had to wait for Junko to leave before he could implement it.

Mayako looked back to Junko and then to Chonnie and Tal'dos in full Rinche gear. Chonnie and Tal'dos looked at each other and then Chonnie said, "We will wait outside."

Tal'dos nodded and said nervously, "Yeah, just to make sure the shadows are in working order."

Chonnie looked at him with a look that said, *Dude!*

Tal'dos ushered him out of the door with an embarrassed look on his face.

Junko put the last of her gear on and walked up to Mayako, "Look Mayako. Things are worse than ever. We don't know what Aniceto and Luis are up to, and we don't know what's going to happen out there. So, please, for once in your life. Listen to your big sister and stay here."

Mayako looked her sister dead in the eye and lied, "Okay I will. But next time, I am coming with you."

Junko patted her on her shoulder and lied, "Sure. Next time."

Mayako watched her sister leave with Chonnie and Tal'dos and plotted what her next move was going to be.

"Mayako, come have some sake with me," Hiro said softly.

Mayako turned around and saw Hiro with the carafe and

two cups set up.

"I'm going home to do some accounting before I meet Naomi tomorrow for the market. Good night, Mayako," Itsuko paused and started to feel a tear form in her eye. "Please be careful. I love you." Then she left without another sound.

Mayako stood stunned. She had never seen her mother so emotional before in her life. She seemed so sad, and she said, I love you. Which she never said to either of them. Something was very wrong.

"Mayako, please sit with me," Hiro gestured for her to the table.

Mayako sat down with her uncle, and they raised their cups and drank down a large swallow of sake. "Oh God, what is that?"

"It's sake. But the good stuff. I made it myself," Hiro said taking another big swallow.

Mayako put the cup down feeling it burn all the way down. "That's okay, Uncle. I'll stick to mezcal."

Hiro closed his eyes and began to sing, *"How can we dance when our earth is turnin'? How do we sleep while our beds are burnin'? How can we dance when our earth is turnin'? How do we sleep while our beds are burnin'?"*

"Uncle, why are you singing that old song?" Mayako interrupted him.

"It's not old," Hiro shot back.

"It's from the 80s. It's old. I was like three." Mayako said annoyed.

"You are so young and full of impatience. I asked you to

stay to give you something. Something that belonged to your grandmother," Hiro said pouring himself another drink.

"Grandma Sakura. You and mamá never really talk about her," Mayako said intrigued.

"That's because she died on the day you were born. Some say her spirit passed to you. You are so much like her. Bullheaded. Passionate. And a Poet," Hiro said feeling the tug at his heart strings remembering her.

"She was a writer too?" Mayako smiled.

"Yes, but she was also a Kampo," Hiro said looking at her.

"A Kampo, is that like a curandera?" Mayako asked.

"Sort of. She had the ability to heal the sick and to see what others couldn't," Hiro poured another drink for both of them.

"Like me?" Mayako said feeling a sense of excitement.

"Yes, very much so," Hiro said sliding an old journal across the table to her. "This was your grandmother's journal. She recorded all her healing practices and her spells."

Mayako scooped it up and began to peruse it. "Crap. I don't read Japanese too well. Junko is much better at that."

Hiro then slid another, newer journal across the table to her, "This is the English translation. As best as I could."

Mayako smiled and said, "Thank you, Uncle."
"Now, I know you are going to follow them out there. I can't in good conscience let you go without protection," Hiro said getting up and opening a chest.

Mayako followed him and looked down to see a ninja uniform.

Aniceto sat on his horse at the old refilling station. He pulled out his pocket watch, the one that his late wife had given his daughter. He rubbed the glass and thought about what brought him here. So much loss. But now they were fighting back. This plan had to work, or he didn't know what he was going to do.

Luis sat next to Aniceto reveling in the fact that he was finally getting somewhere in defeating the Americans and the Rinches. This meeting with El Rinche, if it works, would bring this hero into their fold and then they would be unstoppable. El Rinche commanded so much respect with la gente. A respect that the sediciosos hadn't gained yet. He needed that respect and with the plan coming, they would have it, at last.

"The time has come to say fair's fair. To pay the rent, to pay our share. The time has come, a fact's a fact. It belongs to them, let's give it back," Luis sang as he waited.

"Penny for your thoughts," came El Rinche's voice from the shadows.

Aniceto smiled and said, "Glad you could meet us, Rinche." Aniceto had not revealed his true identity to anyone, not even Luis. He didn't fully trust he wouldn't betray Chonnie.

"Pizaña, you said you had a proposition for us. I'm all ears," El Rinche said stepping from the shadows. Tal'dos stood in the background. His rifle locked into a ready position but pointed downward.

"There are too many beds burning, Rinche. How do we sleep while our beds are burnin'? How can we dance when our earth is turnin'? How do we sleep while our beds are burnin'? Our beds, not those pinche Gringos. Us. Mexicano Tejanos. This is our land. They are killing us by the dozens," Luis preached.

"I know. That's why I do what I do," El Rinche replied.

"It's not enough. Not anymore," Aniceto said.

"Then what do you have in mind?" El Rinche asked.

"A revolution," Luis answered.

Junko was far from the meeting with the sediciosos. She was at a makeshift refueling station turned hideout for the sedicosos. She was looking for anything as to what they were planning when she heard a noise. It was Bennie. He was dressed in a suit and had a thick mustache, which seemed too full for his age. He also had a messenger bag and a stack of papers. He then walked out and jumped on a horse and began to trot off.

Junko went to the table where he had grabbed the papers and saw a document that said:

El Plan De San Diego

On February 20, 1915, at 2:00 there would occur an uprising against the United States government to proclaim the liberty of blacks from the "Yankee tyranny" that had held them in "iniquitous slavery since remote times" and to proclaim the independence of Texas, New Mexico, Arizona, Colorado, and California, "of which States the REPUBLIC OF MEXICO was robbed in a most perfidious manner by North American imperialism."

(2) To achieve these objectives an army would be formed under the leadership of commanders named by the

Supreme Revolutionary Congress of San Diego, Texas. This army, known as the "Liberating Army for Races & Peoples," would fight under a red and white banner bearing the inscription "Equality & Independence".

She didn't need to read anymore. She picked it up and stuff it under her vest.

"Who are you? What are you doing here?" said a sedicioso with his gun in his hand.

Junko, disappointed that a simple pistolero got the drop on her said, "Jesus, I didn't realize I was that rusty. Oh well." She pulled her Escrima sticks from their holsters and in a flash was on the pistolero. She struck the gun from his hand and landed a strike across his temple causing him to collapse to the floor unconscious. Then she jumped back into the shadows and was gone.

Mayako had kept her distance from Junko as she snuck around the sediciosos camp. She watched from a ledge when she saw Bennie in disguise walk out and jump on a horse. But he wasn't alone. She noticed that la Anciana was with him, in disguise as an older Mexicano. Mayako decided to follow him and was surprised when she heard Bennie talking to la Anciana calling him, "Papá."

EL RINCHE

RUNAWAY TRAIN

"This is a runaway train now. Plans are already in motion, Rinche," Luis said feeling he had an upper hand.

El Rinche mulled over the Revolución that they were planning. It seemed an impossible task. The United States would never let them take back the Southwest. The military would crush them. "A lot of good people will get hurt with your plan," El Rinche responded.

"They are already getting hurt. Things are spinning out of control. They killed Jesús Bazan," Aniceto pleaded.

"You're talking about all-out war with the United States. There is already a war brewing in Europe, and the U.S. won't be long behind. Do you think they will bat an eye at a little rebellion by Mexicans? They will crush it without reservation, and all the people that I have been trying to protect will get caught in the wake. Is that what you want?" El Rinche plead with Aniceto and Luis.

"There are always causalities in war. That's the nature of the beast," Luis said callously.

Aniceto gave Luis a side glance and said, "We will be taking the fight to them. We will limit the causalities as best as we can."

"How do you plan to do that? You would have to raise an army in the thousands to do what you are talking about," El Rinche asked.

"We will. After tomorrow, they will hear the rallying cry," Luis said.

"What's happening tomorrow?" El Rinche asked.

"We can't tell you that until you tell us if you are in or not," Luis said.

El Rinche gritted his teeth and fought the urge to lodge a throwing star in Luis' eye. "I can't. I'm sorry, Aniceto. I will continue to protect the people from the rinches, but I can't be involved in this."

El Rinche stepped back into the shadows and was gone.

"I told you he wouldn't be a part of this," Aniceto said to Luis.

"It was worth a shot. Let's prepare to head to San Diego. We have a revolution to plan," Luis said turning his horse and riding away. Aniceto gritted his teeth and followed.

Back in Kondo, Chonnie emerged from the shadows. He removed his mask while Junko laid out the Plan de San Diego on their main hideout table. "They have gone crazy. This is a proclamation of war against the United States," Junko explained.

"You can only poke a man in the chest so many times before he pokes back," Hiro said as he perused the Plan.

"I know their pain, I do. But this cannot be the answer," Chonnie said.

"This war did not spring up on our land. This war was brought upon us by the children of the Great Father who came to take our land without a price, and who, in our land, do a great many evil things… This war has come from robbery – from the stealing of our land. Spotted Tail said that when they came for us," Tal'dos said.

"So, you think we should fight with them?" Chonnie asked.

"No, it's destined to fail. I have seen it. This war has to be stopped at all costs. Because the military is coming and nothing good every comes from the U.S. Army getting involved," Tal'dos said.

"So, what do we do?" Chonnie asked.

"We have to rescue Bennie," Mayako said running into the hideout. "Bad things are coming if we don't. We need Inez."

Inez sat at her working table in her living room. She was down to only fifty heads of cattle left. The beef business was being taken over by the Anglos and since she had sold most of her lands to Stillwell, she was barely making it. She had to lay off half of her vaqueros. Inez had even had to sell her cattle at half of what they were worth. She sighed and set her pen down. She sat back in her chair and felt two hands begin to massage her shoulders. She smiled and said, "That feels good."

Chonnie reached over and kissed her on the cheek. "How are you?"

"It's getting worse. I will have to sell the business before long if this violence gets any worse. I don't have the men to keep it going, but that is neither here nor there. How is the superheroing going?" Inez said.

"Well, that's why I'm here. We need you," Chonnie said.

Inez stood up and faced Chonnie, "Why? What's going on?"

"We have found Bennie, but we need you to bring him back to us," Chonnie said.

"Of course, what do I have to do?" Inez said feeling a sharp kick in her stomach.

Chonnie saw her wince and move her hands to her stomach. "Are you alright?" Chonnie said rushing her into his arms.

"She is fine," Señora García said bringing a platter of coffee and cups. "Está embarazada."

Chonnie felt his throat go dry as he caught her gaze, "Pregnant?"

Señora García set the tray down and said, "I will let you two talk." Then she left the room.

"It's true. I am," Inez said with trepidation.

"That's great. I mean, that's amazing. We are going to have a child," Chonnie continued ecstatic.

"Chonnie, there's more," Inez said.

"What more?" Chonnie asked.

"I can't have this child like this. I am a Catholic and I am unmarried. This is not good," Inez said.

"Well, I will marry you then," Chonnie said not really thinking about what he was saying.

"We can't. You are dead. How are we going to explain any of this?" Inez said.

"I don't know, but…" Chonnie searched for a solution.

"You would have to stop being El Rinche and come back to life," Inez said knowing he couldn't do that.

Chonnie looked her in the eyes and felt the existential terror of the truth, "Then what do we do?"

"I don't know," Inez said truly feeling lost. "Maybe I don't have this child."

Chonnie felt the anger rising in him, "No. No. There has to be another way. I love you. I want our child."

"I want this baby too. I wish there was way, but you can't stop being El Rinche. Not now. Not with things this bad," Inez said feeling her heart sink as she said it.

Chonnie felt desperate. He wanted to marry Inez. To have that life that he thought he was going to have as a lawyer, but that was impossible now. That train had run away from him. "No matter what happens, we are having this child. I don't care what the rest of the world thinks."

"If the rinches know you are alive, they will come for us. This rancho. You know that," Inez said.

"I don't care. I will protect you," Chonnie said feeling the room spinning.

"You can't. You wouldn't be able to fight on all those fronts. You know that," Inez said as quickly as possible.

"Then what do we do?" Chonnie said feeling like he needed something stronger than coffee.

"If I was to give up the rest of our lands. No one will care about an unwed mother. I will no longer be a Doña," Inez said feeling the weight of that proposition.

Chonnie closed his eyes and began to sing under his breath, *"Runaway train never going back. Wrong way on a one-way track. Seems like I should be getting somewhere. Somehow, I'm neither here nor there."*

"I don't want any of this either, but that might be our only choice," Inez said feeling the tears traveling down her cheeks.

Chonnie turned and hugged her hard, "I'm so sorry. For all of this. The one thing I can do is get Bennie back for you. He is my nephew and I owe it to you and Macario."

Inez felt that since they were in a vulnerable space, she would finally tell him the truth. "Well, about Bennie."

"What about him?" Chonnie asked still holding her close.

"He's your son," Inez blurted out.

Chonnie pulled away from Inez dumbfounded. "Bennie is what?"

I can go where no one else can go
I know what no one else knows
Here I am, just drowning in the rain
With a ticket for a runaway train

DAY IN THE LIFE

Bennie rose to a chilly January morning. He was staying at La Casa de Palmas. The fancy new hotel used primarily by the gringos moving into these border communities. They had started calling this area the Río Grande Valley. Even though there were no mountains. They thought it would be more enticing to Anglos to come here to settle. It was what the sediciosos were fighting against. To bring these lands back to Mexico. To free the Southwest from the wrongful occupation by the United States.

"Today is the day. I feel it in the winds. In the chill," Macario said, staring out the window.

"I am ready. This is my moment," Bennie said as he shaved the stubble on his face, leaving only a small mustache. "I am Basilio Ramos. I am a recruiter for la causa."

"Who is Basilio Ramos anyway?" Macario asked.

"No one really. Just an identity we created to do this one thing. We even planted past arrest records and everything. He will be known as B.R. García for today's purposes," Bennie said adjusting his tie.

"That's right, son. This war starts with you at the lead. Forget Luis and Aniceto. You are the true leader of this revolución. We will take back what is ours," Macario whispered in his ear.

Bennie smiled and grabbed his satchel.

Mayako watched him from across the street on the second floor of a tienda that sold boots and belts and such. She had snuck in late last night and watched La Anciana whisper in his ear. She didn't know what La Anciana was telling him, but Mayako knew that she was disguised as Bennie's father. "None of this is good, Uncle," Mayako said to Hiro who had fallen asleep in a chair.

"Yes, yes, more sake," Hiro murmured under his breath.

"Uncle, wake up. He is leaving," Mayako yelled at him.

Hiro awoke with a start and gripped the wooden cane in his hand, "What?"

"He's leaving. We have to do something," Mayako said.

"We can't. We have to wait for the potion to cook. It won't be ready for several hours," Hiro said looking over at a cooking pot on a makeshift stove. It was quietly simmering.

"Then what do we do, Uncle?" Mayako said in desperation.

"We wait for the gang," Hiro said rising from his chair and stretching.

Mayako, clearly frustrated, shrugged and said, "I'm following him. You stay here and watch the potion."

And before Hiro could protest, she was out the door. Hiro looked at the pot and then pulled out a flask and took a swig.

"Did everyone know?" Chonnie said feeling like a fool.

"I think so," Tal'dos said.

Chonnie looked around the room with Inez, Junko, Tal'dos, and Itsuko. They all nodded yes and Chonnie couldn't believe it.

"It's simple math," Tal'dos said as he loaded his rifle.

"I'm sorry I didn't tell you earlier, but I just didn't know how," Inez said as she grabbed a dagger from the arms wall and stuffed it into her boot.

"He looks just like you," Junko said, "And just as terco, too."

Chonnie couldn't believe that his friends never told him something so important. "We will deal with this later. Now, we need to go over the plan."

"They are going to arrest him today. We will have to rescue him tonight from the jail cell," Tal'dos said.

"Good ol' fashion jailbreak," Junko added.

"What do I do?" Inez asked.

"You will have to convince him to come with us," Chonnie said.

"And if he resists?" Inez asks.

"Then you will use your powers of persuasion to make him, or we will knock him over the head and bring him in," Tal'dos said.

"Agreed," Inez nodded.

Just then the door creaked open, and Naomi walked in, "What's going on in here?"

"Naomi," Junko smiled and went over to hug her.

"Hey girl, it's good to see you," Naomi greeted her. "You guys gonna do some superheroing?"

Inez stepped forward and hugged her, "We are finally going to get my Bennie."

"You guys need any help?" Naomi asked.

"No, we got this, but Itsuko could sure use you," Tal'dos nodded at Itsuko.

Itsuko walked up to Naomi, "Yes, we should get to the market before we lose the morning."

"Alright, but y'all be careful out there. It's getting more and more dangerous," Naomi said.

Junko grabbed her hand and led her outside to chat.

"So, tell me about your preacher lover," Junko joked with Naomi.

"He's nice for a white man. He's really trying to help us black folk here. And he ain't too bad in the sack," Naomi laughed a lot.

"Is it serious?" Junko asked.

Naomi smiled and blushed, "I think so, but something is holding him back. I don't know what."

"Give it time. He will see what a badass black mamba you are," Junko said.

"How are things going with your mama? I know you been frosty with her," Naomi said.

"I know you and mamá are close, but it's going to take time. They lied to me about my father, and they still aren't telling me everything," Junko said frustrated.

"Mothers and daughters. I know all about that. Ain't never pretty. But you got a good one, not like mine was," Naomi said grabbing her hands. "Where are you all going today?"

"McAllen, trying to foil another plot that will only bring more death and pain," Junko answered.

"Another day in the life, huh?" Naomi said.

Bennie walked to Andres Villareal's General Store in downtown McAllen. He was here to sell the revolución to him.

"Hola, ¿Cómo estás? Soy B.R. García. I am here for your help," Bennie smiled.

"What kind of help are you looking for?" Andres looked at him suspiciously.

"You are a respected man in this town, and I know you could gather some men for la causa," Bennie said slyly.

"What causa?" Andres said not liking where this was going.

"Revolucíon, mi amigo. Revolucíon against the Gringo. We are building an army to take back what is ours," Bennie said with a smile.

"Sedicioso, I want nothing to do with this. Get out," Andres said pointing toward the front door.

Bennie got the reaction he was waiting for. He knew Andres would not join the causa. He was too much of a vendido. Bennie tipped his hat and walked out.

Jacob walked the streets of downtown McAllen looking to get supplies for a new church he was trying to establish in Hidalgo County. After he had gathered some wood and building supplies onto his truck, he noticed something strange. He saw Ol'

Scratch talking with an old Indian woman in front of Villareal's General Store. Then a young man walked out of the store. Both of them followed the young man and Jacob felt his heart drop to his stomach. "No," he said to himself, "not another one."

Jacob thought he better warn the young man about deals with Ol' Scractch, but a young gringo with a sheriff's badge walked up to the boy first.

"Hey boy, what are you doing?" Todd Mayfair said to Bennie.

"None of your business, rinche," Bennie responded.

"What was you doing in there?" Todd asked suspicious.

"Shopping," Bennie answered coyly.

"Stuff it beaner, I was just called from Mr. Villareal about a greaser like you trying to stir up trouble," Todd said with his hand on his gun.

"I'm not doing anything illegal, deputy. I'm just shopping," Bennie said.

"You're coming with me. You are under arrest," Todd said.

Jacob saw this was going to turn real ugly, so he decided to step in. "Wait. Wait there, officer. He wasn't doing anything. He was just walking. Maybe we can talk about this before things get out of control."

"Preacher, this ain't your concern," Todd said to Jacob. "Just go about your business, or I'm gonna have to arrest you for interfering in the duties of an officer of the law."

"Please, officer…" Jacob tried to talk to him again.

"It's alright, Preacher. I will go with this deputy. I ain't got nothing to hide," Bennie said. Bennie held his hands up to Todd ready to be handcuffed.

Todd smiled and slapped the cuffs on his wrists.

Jacob looked down the block and saw Ol' Scratch tipping his hat at him.

"Just another day in the life, Preacher. Just another day in the life," Bennie said as Todd dragged him away.

FATHER AND SON

It's not time to make a change
Just relax, take it easy
You're still young, that's your fault
There's so much you have to know
Find a girl, settle down
If you want you can marry
Look at me
I am old, but I'm happy
I was once like you are now
And I know that it's not easy
To be calm
When you've found something going on
But take your time, think a lot
Why, think of everything you've got
For you will still be here tomorrow
But your dreams may not

"Is it time for that same old song?" Ol' Scratch said to La

Anciana. They sat at a chessboard. Anciana played white and Ol' Scratch played black.

"It's always that time. These stories are always about fathers and sons. Legacy," La Anciana responded. Pawn to pawn.

"All the pieces are in play. They will surely be at each other's throats any time now," ol' Scratch said. Bishop takes pawn.

"Don't underestimate these heroes. They have a seer and a witch amongst them," La Anciana said. Bishop takes rook.

Ol' Scratch leaned in and studied the board, "What game are you playin' at, vieja?" Knight takes bishop.

"The only game that matters. Good versus evil," La Anciana said countering his knight with her own.

Ol' Scratch laughed and said, "Which one are you? And which am I?"

La Anciana smiled at him and they both laugh.

"You know, Basilio," Todd said with deep complementation, "all you Mexicans think you better than the white man. Well, you ain't. Can't even rely on one of your own. Villarreal turned on you the first chance he got."

Bennie had to swallow his desire to break free from his restraints and beat him to death, but he stayed cool and just allowed Todd to take him to jail.

Todd slammed him into the only cell in the McAllen jail and laid his satchel on his desk. Spilling all the documents out. Todd picked up one of the proclamations, "The Plan de San Diego. What is that?"

Bennie looked at Todd raising his still handcuffed hands to him. Todd came over with a key and Bennie stuck his hands through the only slit in the barred door. He uncuffed him, "What's your name, anyway?"

"My name is Basilio Ramos," Bennie answered maintaining his cover. "You can't hold me here. I haven't done anything wrong."

"Well, this here document says that you want to overthrow the U.S. government. I think that's reason enough," Todd said raising the Plan up to Bennie's face.

"I thought you were a rinche? Why are you wearing a sheriff's badge?" Bennie asked.

"I'm a sheriff when it suits me," Todd said smiling, "Now, I'm gonna leave you here until the judge is ready to see you in the morning. Behave yourself."

Bennie sat down on the thin mattress of the cot bolted to the wall. He looked up through the makeshift window with bars and smiled. Everything was going according to plan.

Bennie leaned his head back and drifted off to sleep.

"Queen to Knight 7," came Mayako's voice behind La Anciana.

La Anciana smiled and looked up to see that Ol' Scratch was gone, "I was wondering when we would meet again."

"I thought you could see the future," Mayako responded pulling a dagger from her belt.

"I can't see the future. That's not my power. Why don't you ask your friend, the Longeye. He's got the sight," La Anciana answered moving her knight to take the Queen.

"What have you done to Bennie?" Mayako said stepping from behind La Anciana.

"Mayako, you could have been a great bruja, but instead you chose to be a reporter. Such a waste of your talents," La Anciana said looking the board over for her next move.

"I am what I choose to be. Now tell me, what have you done?" Mayako said.

"You can't stop it now. Things are already in motion," La Anciana said. "Now, I know you think that magic dagger will kill me, but I have survived so much worse than a little girl with a knife."

Mayako looked down at her dagger and said, "Why are you haunting Bennie with his father?"

"El Rinche must die and what a better story than son against father. It's a tale as old as time," La Anciana smiled.

"Well, I won't let that happen," Mayako said sheathing her dagger.

La Anciana laughed and said, "What are you going to do? You don't have the magic to stop me."

"Maybe I don't, but he does," Mayako said looking up to the shadows.

La Anciana's eyes went wide and turned to see Hiro splashing a potion all over her. La Anciana jumped to her feet screaming in agony. "What have you done?"

"We are sending you to a place you deserve to be," Mayako nodded at Hiro.

Hiro grabbed La Anciana by the shoulders and swung her

into the shadows. La Anciana grabbed the edges of the shadows and said, "You think you may have won this, but I am not the demon you should watch out for. He's coming and he will be so much worse." Then she disappeared into the shadows.

Mayako and Hiro looked at themselves satisfied, but then they heard a dark laugh from behind them. They turned to see a black man in a nice suit and a white beard laughing.

"Check mate," said Ol' Scratch as he disappeared.

Bennie woke with a scream. He felt a piece of his soul being torn from him. He turned and looked all around, "Papá, papá!"

But he was nowhere to be found. "Papá! No, don't leave me," he yelled.

"Bennie," came a soft voice from outside the bars, "I'm here. Your mother."

Bennie could feel regret and shame when he saw his mother's face come out of the shadows. "Mamá, what are you doing here?"

"I'm here to bring you home," Inez said fighting the tears from erupting from her eyes.

"I can't. The plan is already working. I have to play my part," Bennie said.

"No, you don't," came the voice El Rinche emerging from the shadows.

"You! What are you doing here?" Bennie said with a deep hate in his words.

"I'm here to bring you home," El Rinche said.

"Bennie, what you are doing is going to get you killed. This isn't the way," Inez pleaded with him.

"Then what's the right way? Letting the gringos kill us and take everything," Bennie shot back at his mother.

"No, we fight," El Rinche said, "and protect the people. La gente is who really matters. Not starting a war with the United States. That's suicide," El Rinche said.

"Protect the people. You let Serafina die. You couldn't even protect her," Bennie accused El Rinche.

"Bennie, that wasn't his fault. I was there. She killed herself," Inez said reaching out her hands through the bars to touch him.

Bennie looked at El Rinche with such fury and hate, "Where were you when my father and my whole family died? Killed by los pinches rinches. Where were you then? We lost everything and you weren't there."

El Rinche stepped forward and opened the cell door. "I was there," El Rinche said removing his mask.

Bennie couldn't believe what he was looking at. His face filled with confusion. "Uncle Chonnie."

It's not time to make a change (Away, away, away)
Just sit down, take it slowly
You're still young, that's your fault (I know)
There's so much you have to go through (I have to make this decision)
Find a girl, settle down (Alone)
If you want you can marry
Look at me (No)

ASHES OF SAN MIGUEL

Did you get your horns or did they give you wings
Either works just as well...

Grant Johnson was many things. He was a bartender. A former U.S. Marshall. He was Creek and Chickasaw. Born into slavery. A runaway. Partner to the great Bass Reeves. But more than anything he was an honorable man and too good of a friend. Even after death. Grant arrived in McAllen, Texas on the unluckiest of nights. He rode in on his Model A motorcar and next to him was a jar filled with ashes. The ashes of Jesús San Miguel. He was another of Grant's partners that had passed on. Nowadays, he found himself burying his old friends, it was the twilight of ol' gunfighters. He was here to spread San Miguel's ashes along the Río Grande. Jesús was originally from Hidalgo, along the Río Grande. He left home when he was just a child. His family had left to find work in the big factories in East Texas. That's where Jesús San Miguel fell in with Grant Johnson. They were partners in the last years of Grant's tenure as a Marshall. He never had family. He only had Grant and

95

the bar.

"You know Grant, I ain't been home in 30 years. Not since we left when I was a kid," Jesús said sitting at Grant's bar in Houston.

"Are you planning a trip back home?" Grant told him while polishing a beer mug.

Jesús looked up at Grant and with a tear forming in his left eye said, "I ain't got much time left, Grant. I am not gonna make it back. Not while I am breathing. I need you to do me one last favor."

"What is that?" Grant said.

"When I'm gone. I want you to go to Hidalgo and visit a woman I used to know. She was the one that got away. Her name is Gloria Treviño or at least it used to be. I heard she married old Nestor García. So, you might want to look for Gloria García. She was one hellava cook. But anyway, tell her that I never stopped loving her. I want you to cremate me and spread my ashes in the Río Grande. I came from the river, I should return," Jesús said taking the last drink from his glass.

Grant just nodded and thought about serendipity. That was where Bass' girl and adopted son were. Fighting the white man and their progress. Was he being drawn back there for a reason?

"Hey! Get off the road," came the voice of a white man banging on the hood of his car.

Grant was pulled from his thoughts and saw a group of white men with guns and lanterns heading toward the center of town. Grant knew exactly what this was. It was a lynching. Grant pulled his car onto the side of Main Street. He left the ashes of San Miguel in the front seat. He grabbed his shotgun from the trunk and his six shooter. He hadn't had to shoot anybody since his bar was attacked back in Austin.

"Grant, what are you doing here?" Tal'dos said appearing next to him.

"Tal'dos, right now I'm here to stop bad men from doing a bad thing," Grant said getting his game face on.

"Don't worry. There's not going to be a lynching here tonight. We got this covered," Tal'dos said pulling Duyukdu to his shoulder and fired a shot in the air.

Jacob Freeman saw what was going to happen here tonight before the men gathered their guns, and headed for a midnight meeting to take care of Basilio Ramos. He knew they were out for blood and who better than a Mexican recruiting for a revolution. Jacob couldn't let that happen. He heard a shot go off. It didn't come from the crowd. The shot whizzed into the sky. Jacob wasted no time. He made his way to the jail as the crowd began to approach. There he saw Todd again. He never could seem to get rid of this kid. He first met him on the road to becoming Jacob. Ever since he had become Jacob the kid never recognized him. It must have been the crossroads deal. "Please, listen to me. You don't want to do this," Jacob plead.

"Preacher, get out of the way," said Todd Mayfair leading the mob.

"This isn't the way. We have to let the justice system do its work," Jacob said trying to calm the horde.

"Preacher, I know you think you are doing the Christian thing, but he's just a Mexican," another man shouted from the crowd.

Todd raised his rifle and said, "Now, get out of our way or we gonna have to shoot you down."

Jacob didn't know what to do. He was desperate, but he had no choice. The crowd pushed him aside and entered the city jail.

"I told you. You can't stop a bad man from doing a bad thing. Especially a white man with an audience," Ol' Scratch said from behind Jacob.

"This isn't the way it was supposed to be," Jacob hung his head low as the last of the mob entered the jail.

"He ain't here," Todd shouted in disappointment.

Jacob lifted his head and smiled.

"See, sometimes things work out for themselves," Ol' Scratch said.

Jacob turned to look at Ol' Scratch standing in the shadows. "I don't want this deal anymore."

"That ain't up to you no more. You signed the contract. Ain't no way out now," Ol' Scratch said sounding a bit annoyed.

Jacob watched as the crowd left the jail upset. There wasn't going to be a lynching and the crowd seemed restless, but decided to disperse. He looked back to where Ol' Scratch used to be and clenched his fists.

"What have I done?" Jacob said.

"You lost?" Ol' Scratch said to a weathered and worn preacher driving a black truck. The preacher was standing at the crossroads. He was deciding which direction to go.

The weathered preacher looked at him. "We are heading to South Texas. Do you know which is the right way?"

"Oh Pablo, of course I know," Ol' Scratch said, "The question is do you?"

"How do you know that name?" the weathered preacher said surprised and shook.

"I know a lot about you. The question is what do you want?" Ol Scratch said.

"I want to leave all that behind. I want to be Jacob Freeman. I want to be a good man," the weathered preacher spilled all his desires to this stranger at a crossroads.

"And you can have all that. A prosperous church, a nice woman by your side, and you can be Jacob Freeman. No more Pablo Honey. No more Man Who Lost His Name. I can give you all that," Ol' Scratch smiled at him.

"Really? How?" the weathered preacher said skeptical.

"I can make this face permanent, and no one will see who you ever were. All you got to do is sign away the one thing you ain't gonna need," Ol' Scratch proposed.

"You the devil, and I'm going to bargain my soul for a better life. Is that what you are offering?" the weathered preacher said sarcastically.

"I ain't the devil, but you ain't far off. You know you want this," Ol' Scratch said stretching his hand out for shaking.

The weathered preacher looked at Ol' Scratch's hand and said, "No one's going to know who I was?"

"No, but there is a caveat," Ol' Scratch said.

"I knew it. What is it?" the weathered preacher scoffed at Ol' Scratch.

"You can't pick up the guns again. Not ever. Or the deal is off and everyone gonna know who you really are," Ol' Scratch said with a tone that screamed serious.

The weathered preacher shook his hand, and he felt a prick in his palm. He pulled away.

Ol' Scratch smiled and said, "All deals must be signed in blood."

Tal'dos stood with Junko and Grant on the top of the city jail watching the mob disperse.

"It worked," Junko said. "Chonnie and Inez have Bennie. They are already heading back to Kondo."

"Good," Tal'dos said then saw a weathered preacher walking from the jailhouse steps. He looked so familiar, but he couldn't quite place him. Then he saw Naomi embracing him and taking him away. Tal'dos felt a cold wind blow and he saw the future and the past at the same time. "Oh no. It can't be."

Hiro sat back at the hideout reading through his mother's diaries when he felt a cold wind blow. "I have been waiting for you," Hiro said gripping his cane tightly.

"Hiro, it's been a long time," a shadowy figure dressed in full ninja gear stepped from the shadows.

"Not long enough, Atoy," Hiro said rising to his feet.

"You know why I'm here. It's time to pay the piper," Atoy said removing his mask and revealing Junko and Mayako's father's face.

EL RINCHE

NOTHING MAN

Once divided...nothing left to subtract...
Some words when spoken...can't be taken back...
Walks on his own...with thoughts he can't help thinking...
Future's above...but in the past, he's slow and sinking...
Caught a bolt 'a lightnin'...cursed the day he let it go...

"I can't do what you are asking, Jovita," J.T. said from behind his desk.

"J.T., we go back a long ways. You are just as affected by what's going on out there as the rest of us," Jovita said exhausted by his dismissive tone.

"What do you want me to do? I have no jurisdiction in Laredo. I am a lawyer here in Brownsville," J.T. stood up and looked out of his office window. He was tall and light skinned and dressed in a sharp grey pinstriped suit. Glasses on the edge of his nose.

"You used to be a legislator. You could run again and take down these rinches," Jovita said watching him look out the window.

She wondered if Chonnie's path had taken a different turn, would this have been him?

"I am the county superintendent of public schools now. I don't wish to go back to that cesspool of Texas law," J.T. said bitterly.

"You have always been a political animal, J.T. Sitting back and playing it safe when your people need you is…" Jovita stumbled before she completed that thought.

"…cowardly," J.T. finished her thoughts.

"Well, that's not exactly the word I was going to use, but yes," Jovita said sheepishly.

"Do you know how they used to introduce me on the legislative floor?" J.T. asked.

Jovita stayed quiet knowing the answer.

"'The greaser from Brownsville.' Not the distinguished gentleman from Brownsville, but the greaser from Brownsville. That's what they think about me there. Even though I was the youngest graduate from law school at University of Michigan. I was twenty-two. Twenty-two. And yet because I am a Canales and have Mexican lineage, I am the greaser from Brownsville," J.T. said turning back to Jovita.

"J.T., I'm sorry, but I can't feel sorry for you. I have been the target of an assassination attempt, my press has been burned down, and I am a woman standing up to the rinches. Yet, I am still in the fight. We need you now more than ever," Jovita said with a fire she had not felt since before they burned down her press.

"Jovita, I respect everything you do, but I cannot get

involved," J.T. said picking up a cigar from the box on his desk.

"Will you at least meet with El Rinche? Hear from someone fighting the good fight," Jovita threw one last Hail Mary.

"The vigilante that has been stirring up trouble," J.T. scoffed at the meeting.

"He has been protecting the people, and he saved my life. He is a hero," Jovita shot back. "If it makes you feel any better, you can meet at Inez's."

J.T. lit his cigar and said, "Inez Plata, huh?"

"I know you respect her and her family. She's having a gathering at her house this Friday. It would be perfect cover," Jovita posited.

"Okay, I will go," J.T. said.

"He's a Nothing Man, mijo. A Nothing Man. He did nothing to save your girl. He has your mother under a spell," Macario said as he sat under a mesquite tree. Fire crackling in the night. Bennie was cooking a rabbit on a spit while the coffee boiled in its pot.

"But who is he? This mysterious figure," Bennie asked the ghost of his father.

"He's a demon. He needs to die. Like the rest of them. A white man thinking he can save us from ourselves," Macario scoffed.

"But..." Bennie stumbled feeling a wave of déjà vu come over him. "Haven't we done this before? Had this conversation?"

Bennie turned to look at his father who now wasn't his

father. He looked like a Japanese man dressed all in black. "Wait. Who are you?"

The man in black laughed and said, "I'm your father. Who else would I be?" He then shifted back into Macario.

Relieved, Bennie turned back to the spit, "I remember the story you used to tell me about el Hombre Nada. The man who did nothing and was nothing. He was destined to be forgot. That is why I had to be Algo Hombre. To make a difference in the world like Tío Chonnie."

Bennie turned to where his father was. He was gone and then the fire disappeared. He was now surrounded by darkness. It began to swallow him. Bennie could feel it squeezing him and then he awoke to find himself in his bed. He looked around frantically and recognized his old room. It took him a minute to remember what had happened. Then the anger filled him.

Gloria had not thought of Jesús San Miguel in years. He was the one that got away. He was the young vaquero that worked the Plata ranch when she was just a maid working with her mother. She was sixteen. He was seventeen. It was first love. That kind of love that is so innocent. So passionate. So tender. Then like all first loves. He was gone. His family left for Houston. They stayed in touch by letter until the letters eventually stopped.

"Gloria. I am an old friend of Jesús'. We rode together back when we were lawmen," Grant said.

"He's gone. Isn't he?" Gloria asked him knowing the answer.

"Yes, he asked me to tell you that he never stopped loving

you," Grant said.

Gloria felt the tears welling up. "Thank you for telling me."

Grant had never had the sight. Not like his mother. She could sense when bad things were coming. Grant always relied on his instincts when trouble was coming, but at this moment, something happened. He felt the winds shift and for the first time in his life he heard it. The sky cracked and he heard it. Grant looked around and grabbed his gun from his holster. "Get inside."

"What's happening?" Gloria said wiping the tears from her face.

"There's evil coming," Grant said.

Then a shot rang out and Grant turned to the house. He saw Bennie running out the front door with a gun in his hand.

EL RINCHE

EVIL IS ALIVE AND WELL

It doesn't always have a shape
Almost never does it have a name
It maybe has a pitchfork maybe has a tail
But evil is alive and well
It might walk upright from out of the inferno
May be coming horseback through deep snow
It's ragged fat and fat, it's hungry as hell…

Atoy rode the last boat out of Manila. He had just witnessed the latest in the atrocities of the Spanish on his people. Gomburza. Garroted in the public square for everyone to see. The Spanish were ruthless even to their own. Three priests who spoke out for the Filipinos, killed for speaking the truth. Isn't that how it always was? Atoy had been there when it had all started. He was in Sampaloc celebrating with his brother and sisters the Feast of the Virgin of Loreto. He watched as the dancers took to the stage. They were doing their big number and when the big climax exploded into a series of fireworks in the sky, everyone cheered. Atoy remembered how happy they all were. He turned to his sister and saw blood gushing from her neck. She grasped it but it was too late. She fell over and then the screams and the gunshots. The crowd pushed him away from his family. It was a human wave so strong, he didn't remember anything after he was kicked in the head. The morning light woke him to hundreds of bodies shot dead. They called it a revolt by those shot dead.

The fireworks, they said, sounded like canons. They accused the natives of seizing the arsenal and starting an uprising. Atoy was now a revolutionary. The only ones who stood for the truth were the three priests. Gomburza, they were called. It was a word the natives called them. Their names smashed together. Fathers Mariano Gomez, Jose Burgos and Jacinto Zamora. Filipinos loved their nicknames. The Spanish didn't like their narrative of the Revolt challenged, so they charged and convicted the three priests for leading it. Their real crime was hosting a feast for the natives. Atoy was in the crowd when he saw the three men. They weren't shot or hung. They were garroted with a thin wire. A sight so gruesome he couldn't ever get that image out of his mind. So, he packed his Escrima sticks and jumped the first boat out of Manila. It was heading for Japan.

May be too humble to want to speak
May have a blood soaked bird in it's teeth
Smoked filled skies and bees in the well
Evil is alive and well
Maybe in a palace it may be in the streets

May be here among us on a crowded beach
May be asleep in a roadside motel
But evil is alive and well…

Atoy awoke for his job as the blacksmith for the village. He looked over to see that his Itsuko was already up and attending to their newborn, Mayako. She was so small. Nothing like their first born, Junko, who at four years old was already playing with her father's Escrima sticks and learning martial arts from her uncle. This was the happiest he had been in years. He was a stranger in a strange land, but Itsuko never made him feel that way. Even with his broken Japanese and his thick accent. Itsuko would only smile when he stumbled and kiss him on the lips and say, "The words will come."

Itsuko had already packed his lunch. He grabbed up his pail and walked out into the bright sky. It wasn't a long walk to his shop, but when he got there a sense of dread filled him. He saw Hattori Hanzō standing there. He had at least ten men with him. Atoy swallowed hard and asked, "How can I help you?"

"Are you Atoy Torres?" Hanzō asked him.

Atoy didn't know where this was going, but he answered, "Yes, that is me. Did you need some weapons or armor mended?"

"No, Atoy, I believe you are married to Itsuko," Hanzō said.

Atoy really didn't like this, "Yes, what is this about?"

"Her brother is Hiro, and his master is Fūma Kotarō," Hanzō continued.

"I don't know anything about that. I don't want to get

involved," Atoy said unlocking his shop door.

"You are already involved. Remember Gomburza," Hanzō said.

Atoy felt his throat go dry and he could hear his heartbeat, "That was a long time ago."

"You are still a wanted fugitive. There is still a warrant out for your arrest," Hanzō said pulling a paper from his breast. He stabbed it into the front door of Atoy's workshop.

"What do you want?" Atoy said sheepishly.

"I need information. You see, there is a war coming, another revolution. And your brother-in-law and his master are deep in the middle of it all. I can't have that. You will be my spy, or you will be shipped back to the Philippines. I hear they are still using the garrot as their primary execution method for traitors," Hanzō said laughing.

Atoy closed his eyes and slowly nodded.

"Good," Hanzō said slapping him on his back. "Oh, we also need our swords sharpened."

Evil is alive
Evil is well
Evil is alive
Evil is well
On your feet to the tower and yell
Evil is alive and well...

Atoy watched as they were all slaughtered. Again. He was

in the middle of another massacre and once again, his family was right there. He didn't know if feeding Hanzō information was the right thing to do, but he had no choice. The garrot waited for him back home. And his wife and children wouldn't understand. This was the life he always wanted. A simple life. Family, children, quiet nights watching the night sky, but the stars were never in his favor. He was cursed to always be in the middle of the worst of mankind.

"Atoy, help," came Itsuko's voice from behind him.

Atoy whipped around and saw Itsuko helping Hiro with a bloodied knee into their house.

"They knew we were coming. How does he always know?" Hiro said beaten and bloodied.

Itsuko laid him down and looked at Hiro's wound. His knee was barely hanging on.

"They say Hanzō has the sight. He can see the future," Atoy said helping Itsuko with water to clean the wound and the herbs of her mother.

"Where are the girls?" Itsuko said frantic.

"They are safe. Hidden in the secret place," Atoy answered.

"Good, now get me those bandages," Itsuko shouted at Atoy.

Atoy went to grab the bandages when the front door burst open and Hattori Hanzō and a couple of his samurai burst in. Weapons drawn.

Hiro tried to sit up, but he was in too much pain.

"Where is he? Where is Fūma Kotarō?" Hanzō shouted.

"He's not here!" Itsuko yelled.

"Arrest them all. This rebellion is finished," Hanzō said.

Atoy stepped forward and said, "No, please don't. My wife and I had nothing to do with this. Please."

Hanzō smiled at Atoy and said, "You have done well, Atoy. You have served your purpose, but how did you think this was going to end?"

Hiro and Itsuko looked at Atoy confused and Itsuko said, "What is he talking about?"

Atoy hung his head low.

Hanzō laughed and said, "Atoy here is the reason your rebellion failed. He has been working for me this whole time."

"Is this true?" Itsuko said shocked.

Atoy looked at her, "You don't understand. I can't go back to the Philippines."

Hiro sat up and said, "You son of a bitch. How could you? Those are your friends out there too."

"I didn't have a choice. He promised me my family would be safe," Atoy said feeling shame drown him.

"Never trust the word of a government stooge. Even if he wears the clothes of a samurai," came a voice from the shadows.

Hanzō smiled and lifted his sword and said, "Kill them all. Fūma Kotarō is mine."

Fūma Kotarō stepped from the shadows, swords in both hands and in full ninja gear. "Leave them out of this. This is between you and me. It always has been."

"Sorry, Fūma, no one gets out of here alive. Especially you," Hanzō said squaring off with Fūma.

Just then a loud pop when off and Hanzō stumbled back a

little. Hanzō turned to see Itsuko holding a Colt .45 pistol. "The next one goes in your face," she said.

Hanzō reached up to where the bullet hit his armor. "Good armor," he smiled.

Atoy saw it first, before anyone. Hanzō flung a shuriken at Itsuko. Atoy didn't know where he summoned the speed, but he ran as fast as he could. The shuriken struck him right in the heart. He knew this was it. His last moments on Earth. Itsuko fell with him to the floor. "Atoy, no," she cried out.

"It's okay, my love. This is the one brave thing I have ever done in my life, and I am glad," he coughed up blood. Atoy could feel the life draining from him.

Fūma Kotarō did not hesitate. He knew the only way to defeat Hanzō, so he summoned the shadows and pushed him into it. The other two samurai rushed toward Hiro and Itsuko, but Hiro fired one shot each into their foreheads. He then dropped the gun and said, "I hate guns."

Atoy smiled as he gazed into his wife's eyes. "I am so sorry." Then all was darkness and stillness.

When midnight's done and the day won't start
And All I ever gave you was a broken heart
It's hard to admit but it's easy to tell
That evil is alive and well...

EL RINCHE

GIMME SHELTER

Nikola Tesla rode the last train out of Manhattan with his last twenty dollars in his pocket. He packed up his inventions and had them shipped to his lawyer. She was the only person he trusted. She lived deep in South Texas on a ranch and said she no longer practiced law, but that would not stop Nikola. He needed her. She always accepted his inventions as payment. And this time, one of his best inventions was being stolen by some hack named Marconi. He claimed to discover how to carry signals through the air. Tesla scoffed. He discovered that years ago. He needed to sue Marconi, but he was out of money. He had lost his laboratory, failure to pay the rent was what the eviction notice said. First Edison, and now Marconi was stealing his work. He had so many ideas, but even he had to admit he was not good at business. That is where Edison always had him beat. Tesla was a man of science, through and through, but even science needs money. He recognized that.

And he was sure that he was being followed. Two men in long black coats had been on him since he left Grand Central Station. He noticed them like he noticed most things, they did not fit. He was able to see the geometry of everything. The way that everything fit in its proper place. Nikola had to make himself fit. Somehow. That is why he always had to have his apartment at exactly 3, 6, and 9 angles or multiples of 3, 6, 9. That was how the world best worked in harmony. These men did not fit those angles and that was why he knew he was being followed. Was it Edison? Marconi? Or the United States? He didn't know. They were always after his inventions. They would not follow him to San Diego, Texas. No, no, no.

Ooh, a storm is threatening
My very life today
If I don't get some shelter
Ooh yeah, I'm gonna fade away...

Ginnie rose from her large European pillowtop mattress and stretched herself awake. It was a gray overcast February morning, and a nip was in the air. She walked over to the window and saw the dawn peeking over the horizon.

"Time to get to work, Ginnie," she said to herself.

Ginnie readied herself and dressed in her vaquero jeans and large sombrero. She checked with her vaqueros as they tended to her cattle. Ginnie had relocated from Austin after los pinches rinches had burned down her home. She took the insurance money and bought this little 10-acre ranch outside of San Diego. She wanted to stay close to the action along the border. She had kept in touch with Inez and Jovita and knew that the violence was out of control. It was even affecting the citizens of Duval County.

The rinches were here too. They were searching for the leaders of the Plan de San Diego. Little did they know that the Plan leaders were holed up in her barn. She was very invested in their plan to take back the Southwest. She had nothing but contempt from the men in the legal field. And the violence she had seen perpetrated on Mexicans was too much to handle through the law since the law was always on the side of the white man.

"Señora Yeager, we need to run into town to get the feed," young Patricio Gonzalez said from a large black truck with wood paneling.

"Sí, Patricio, I am coming," Ginnie said hopping in the passenger seat.

"Los rinches are everywhere," Patricio complained.

"I know. The arrest of Basilio has really caused a stir. Just stay calm and let me deal with it," Ginnie reassured Patricio.

"I heard that we might get involved in the war in Europe. Will I have to fight?" Patricio said sounding concerned.

"No, Patricio, don't worry about that. We have the Revolution to the South and the violence here. Wilson has way too much to deal with to think about getting involved in a war that has nothing to do with us," Ginnie said, not really believing the words she was saying.

Patricio pulled up in front of the feed store and noticed a Ranger harassing two young Mexican workers. She saw the tall white man in his tiny badge pull out his gun and pistol whip one of the Mexican workers. Ginnie's eyes went wide and before she knew it, she was out of the truck and running to the Ranger.

"Hey! Stop that, right now!" Ginnie said.

The Ranger stopped beating the Mexican man and said, "Ma'am, please this is Ranger business. Please step back."

"No, I will not. This man has done nothing. Why are you beating him?" Ginnie said.

"Listen ma'am. This has nothing to do with you. You are a white woman. This is a Mexican man. We are here to protect you," the Ranger said.

"Protect me? From what? From a man going about his business and doing no harm to anyone? I insist you let this man go!" Ginnie said forcefully.

The Ranger seemed rather annoyed with her, so he turned his full attention to Ginnie and said, "Listen here, I am a Texas Ranger…"

"…I know what you are," Ginnie cut him off with disdain.

The Ranger got angry and was about to raise his hand to strike her, but the conviction in her eyes stopped him. The Ranger looked around and saw everyone watching him, so he relaxed. "Fine, I got everything I need from him anyway," he said and began to step back.

"Thank you, sir," Ginnie said as she held his angry eyes in her stare.

The Ranger scoffed and turned and walked away. In the distance, Ginnie could swear she heard him say, "Later, bitch, later."

Ginnie bent down to help the bleeding man off the ground. She apologized to him, and he said he was fine. Ginnie turned back to see the Ranger fade out of her eyeline. She knew now that she had just made herself a target. She would have to cancel the meeting tonight. She had just made her ranch too hot for comfort for the sediciosos'.

War, children
It's just a shot away
It's just a shot away
War, children
It's just a shot away
It's just a shot away
Ooh, see the fire is sweepin'
Our streets today
Burns like a red coal carpet
Mad bull lost its way

The night air was filled with burning sensation that Ginnie couldn't quite taste or smell. It was just there. A tear in the fabric of the universe. She sipped on her Irish Coffee with a bit of canela. It was her nightly nightcap. But this night she wasn't readying herself for bed. She was on high alert. She sat on her front porch in her favorite rocking chair. That Ranger was out for blood. Ginnie knew that she was on his radar now.

Then it came. A click clackity sound from down the road and then bright lights heading toward her house. Ginnie grabbed her rifle and stepped down from her front porch. The truck came to a stop and a young white man jumped from the driver's seat.

"Whoa. Whoa. Whoa. Ms. Ginnie. It's just me Pete," Pete Burrel said with his hands up.

"Pete? What are you doing here this late at night?" Ginnie said lowering her rifle.

"I got a delivery for you from a Nick Tes…something or other," Pete said with his hands still raised.

Ginnie sighed and said, "Nicky Tesla, you weirdo. Yes, just put whatever it is in the barn."

Pete lowered his hands and said, "It's a lot of stuff. I could really use a hand."

Ginnie annoyed by Tesla said, "Sure, Patricio, get some boys out here to help Pete unload all this stuff."

Patricio and some of the other ranch hands we settling down for the night in the makeshift cabins by Ginnie's barn. Patricio poked his head out with a latern in his hand. "Ma'am?" he asked.

"Can you help me with all this?" Ginnie said.

"Of course Señora," Patricio as he pulled on his boots.

After an hour, Ginnie's barn was filled with crates. Of what? She had no idea. Ginnie spent the better part of the night opening them. There was so much scientific equipment that she eventually stopped. She sat on one of the crates and poured herself some more Irish coffee. She didn't know what any of this stuff was doing here. Or what Tesla was up to, but she knew that he would soon show up and rope her into one of his many legal battles.

Then in the night stillness came a cough and a groan. Ginnie jumped to her feet and grabbed her rifle. It came from the corner of her barn. She cautiously made her way to see a dark figure laying on the ground. Ginnie still had her rifle trained on the figure when she got close enough to recognize him.

"Chonnie?" Ginnie said rushing over to him and dropping the rifle. "What are you doing here?"

"Ginnie," Chonnie said weakly, "please gimme…gimme shelter."

Ginnie examined him and saw that he was shot twice. "Why weren't you wearing your vest?"

"Ginnie, I…I…I…" Chonnie said before he collapsed into unconsciousness.

"Well, well, well. If it's not the Good Samaritan," the Ranger's voice came from the open barn door.

Ginnie quickly turned, but her rifle was too far. She stood up and faced the Ranger. He was leaning against the open doorway with his pistol pointed right at her. "You really embarrassed me today. Now, you are going to make it up to me."

"Really, you shouldn't be here. This is private property," Ginnie said with as much as courage as she could muster.

The Ranger stepped forward, he was noticeably drunk, "What is a pretty white woman doing with these Mexicans anyway? You need a good white man."

"I guess you mean you?" Ginnie asked sarcastically.

"You owe me," the Ranger said pulling the trigger back, "and I am going to coll---"

Just then he seized up and blue sparks covered his body as he fell over on the ground.

Ginnie stood there stunned. Then a thin bespeckled scientist with a rubber glove on his hand stepped out of the darkness. "Nicky, I have never been so glad to see you," she said with a sigh of relief.

"Miss Yeager. I need your services. Marconi has stolen my radio designs," Tesla said ignoring the scene around him.

"Of course, Nicky. I am fine by the way," Ginnie said.

Rape, murder, it's just a shot away
It's just a shot away
Rape, murder, yeah, it's just a shot away
It's just a shot away
Rape, murder, it's just a shot away
It's just a shot away

I'M NOT OKAY [I PROMISE]

"Take a breath. It will be okay," said a soft voice.

Bennie could see nothing. It was just darkness and his beating heart, beating faster and faster. He could hear his blood pumping in his veins. It was like the world was gone and he was in The Empty. The place where dead things go to die. "Where are I?" Bennie said struggling with his tongue.

"How deep is the red when blood is turned to rust? How loud the cry of a gunshot? How long is the memory when the ghosts are forgotten? How long can the earth swallow us after we have become ash? How long must pasts sins live until our genes can finally forget?" the soft voice sang.

"Who are you?" Bennie cried out in the Empty.

"I am here for you. That is all you need to know," said the soft voice.

"What is going on?" Bennie asked in desperation.

"This is a cleansing. A limpia. A harai," said the soft voice growing stronger.

"Why do I need a limpia?" Bennie asked looking around

the Empty for the voice which seemed to be getting closer.

"You are filthy. You shot your own father. La Anciana's curse is deep in your bones, it has polluted every aspect of you," said Mayako as she appeared before him dressed in formal Japanese robes.

"Who is La Anciana and who are...wait...I know you," Bennie said looking into Mayako's face.

Mayako smiled and said, "We knew each other once, but you have been lost for so long that you wouldn't know a vaca from a burro's ass."

"What?" Bennie said confused.

"Exactly. Now, let us begin, shall we?" Mayako said extending her hand for Bennie to take.

"What are we beginning?" Bennie asked reluctant to take her hand.

"Your spiritual cleansing," Mayako said sticking her hand out further toward him.

Bennie looked at her looking sweet and innocent and knew she was anything but. He slowly reached out and took her hand. The world swirled around him, and he felt himself falling. The ground grew closer and closer, Bennie screamed.

Aniceto took the back paths to get to Inez's rancho. He was a wanted man now more than ever. It was February 20th, the date that the revolution was supposed to begin, but this was a lie. No matter what the Plan said, they were not ready to launch such an attack. And with Chonnie missing or dead, he needed to talk to

Inez. It was the only way.

Aniceto dismounted his horse in the monte they played in as kids and waited. He went up to the tree where Chonnie and Inez had declared their love. He stared hard at the carved tree truck and ran his finger across the crude engraving.

"That was such as long time ago, Aniceto. We were so young and stupid," Inez said from behind him.

"Simpler times. Before Serafina. Before this…" Aniceto said raising his arm to signal all around him.

"Why are we here, Aniceto?" Inez said sounding annoyed.

"Where is Chonnie?" Aniceto said turning to face Inez. "Is he dead?"

Inez looked at him and burst into tears, "I don't know. He's just gone."

"What happened?" Aniceto asked stepping closer to her and taking her into his arms.

"Bennie shot him and then…he was just gone," Inez said holding Aniceto tighter.

"I knew he blamed El Rinche for Serafina's death, but I didn't know he would shoot his own father," Aniceto said feeling her pain.

"I don't even know where Bennie is now. I just got him back and he ran off again," Inez said, broken.

"I will find him. I will bring him back to you," Aniceto tried to reassure her.

"No, I have to find him. With Chonnie gone. I don't know what I am going to do. I am so tired," Inez said feeling like she was going to fall to pieces.

"Inez," Aniceto said pulling her from his embrace and looking dead into her eyes, "you have always been the heart of this place. We need you to be strong like you always are."

"Why do I always have to be the strong one? Why can't I be the one that stays in bed all day and orders her maids around?" Inez asked.

"Because that is not who you are," Aniceto answered.

"I'm pregnant and Chonnie is gone. What am I going to do?" Inez just blurted it out.

Aniceto looked at her and saw desperation and fear in her eyes and said, "This is Chonnie. He's been dead once before."

Tal'dos awoke with a start. He didn't know what had happened. Everything was different. He turned to look at his bedroom window and saw the moon shining down on him and Junko still asleep.

"What'd you see?" came Hiro's voice from the shadowy corner of his bedroom.

Tal'dos wasn't surprised he was here, "Nothing good. No Chonnie. No end to this matanza. The more I try to see a way out of this, the more I feel like I am falling deeper and deeper into desperation."

"You have to keep looking. There is always hope," Hiro said.

"Tal'dos. Who are you talking to?" Junko said sleepily without opening her eyes.

"Nothing. Go back to sleep," Tal'dos looked to where Hiro was supposed to be and saw nothing.

Bennie and Mayako sat in a movie theater. The only viewers in an empty room. Mayako snacked on popcorn. "They never put enough butter and jalapenos."

"How can you eat popcorn with jalapenos?" Bennie asked.

"It is so good. You have to try it," Mayako said shoving the bucket towards him.

"No thanks," Bennie said looking back at the screen. "What is all this you are showing me?"

"Oh, this is the damage you have done. You think your anger over the death of your girlfriend gives you the right to destroy everyone around you?" Mayako asked.

"My father said…"

"…your father is dead!" Mayako said cutting him off. "He died ten years ago. That thing that was whispering in your ears for the past three years was not your father."

"Apparently my father was not my father," Bennie said looking down.

"So, you shoot your actual father? How did that work out for you?" Mayako said.

"Well…I…I don't know," Bennie said feeling a wave of guilt.

"Mira, put these on," Mayako said handing him a pair of plastic glasses with one red lens and a blue one.

"What are these?" Bennie said taking them from her.

"They are 3-D glasses. So, you can relive your worst mistake in a completly immersive experience," Mayako said already wearing hers.

Bennie hesitated and then he put the glasses on. Suddenly, he was back to that fateful day. The day he awoke in his old bed. It was the day after El Rinche had rescued him from the jail. He saw his mom and his Tío Chonnie talking as he made his way down the stairs.

"Bennie, you are awake," Inez said sounding so happy.

"What is he doing here?" Bennie said with disdain.

"Bennie, this is your Tío Chonnie. Don't you remember?" Inez said trying to make him comfortable.

"Don't you mean my father?" Bennie in the past shot back.

"Well, yes, but…" Inez started to explain.

A cigarette burn flickered in the corner of the living room and Bennie was transported out of the scene.

It was too hot of a day for vengeance, but vengeance is too terco to care. Especially when it is carried by an eighteen-year-old boy whose heart was broken for the first time. The clouds were nowhere to be seen. Not this day. They were comfortable hanging over the beach where it was cool, but out here, in the spina covered brushlands of nowhere between the Pizaña Rancho and the Plata Rancho, there was just heat, dirt and a trail of blood that the land just drank up with its insatiable thirst. The revenge-filled boy had a shiny silver revolver in his hand wet with the sweat. The heat didn't bother him too much, it was the task that had his throat parched. He had his man, El Rinche was going to be dead today. In the middle of nowhere, he had his gun trained on him. El Rinche was propped up against a lone tree. He was covered in bullet holes. His dark hat long lost to the dry winds. Only his mask and those damn green eyes, the boy had him. This man that was the cause of all of his problems. He had him dead to rights, but something stopped him from pulling that trigger. Something deep inside was clawing its way out. Something that he couldn't contain.

"This is for mi Serafina, you sonofabitch," the boy said through gritted teeth.

El Rinche just looked at him, stunned from the multitude of wounds his body was trying to heal. He said nothing to the boy.

"Speak, goddamnit, speak! Tell me why."

El Rinche looked him dead in his anguished green eyes and said, "There ain't nothing I can say that's gonna give you any kind of satisfaction."

"How about the truth? Why don't we start there?" the boy said taking a step closer.

"You don't want the truth."

"Yes, I do. I want to know what happened. What really happened. Why did you kill her?"

"I can't tell you, so your just gonna have to shoot me," El Rinche said trying to sit up more comfortably, but the pain just intensified.

"So, you admit you killed her."

"Son, sometimes things can get so messed up that any explanation will just sound...crazy."

"Just tell me the truth."

"The truth is always more complicated than it sounds."

"Why is that?"

"Because it requires context."

"What the hell are you talking about?"

Then Bennie fired the fatal shot, and the screen went blank.

"That's not what happened," Bennie shouted at the screen.

"Are you sure?" Mayako asked.

"Yes, that's not what happened. I know I was there," Bennie said.

"Then why do you remember it that way?" Mayako asked.

"No, this is all wrong," Bennie said taking the glasses from his face.

The world swirled around him again and he was standing on the side of a road, it was morning. He could see the sun peeking out of the night sky. He looked around and saw a string of trees and railroad tracks.

"What is this?" Bennie shouted at scene.

"Just look," Mayako said as she appeared next to him. She pointed at the line of trees that bore strange fruit.

Fifteen trees Bennie counted. Fifteen men. Dangling like demented fruit. Bennie could do nothing but stand there in horror.

"This is what real evil does," Mayako whispered in his ear.

RESTLESS SINNER

Restless Sinner
Restless sinner rest in sin
He's got no face to hold him in
He fills his days as dark as night
He's been wait'n with the blind
Just to find a place to hide his ghost...

"You know Todd, sometimes the most beautiful times are when the sun peeks out from its hiding place. Its rays cast the light on the awaiting message. Nothing like a string of messages from here to there. Then they see it, and the horror on their faces shows that they know. They know they must obey, or die like them," Hamer said while puffing his cigar.

"Captain Hamer, sir, I am done. What do I do now?" Todd said securing the last of the unlucky dead from the unlucky tree.

"Ain't you heard a thing I said, Todd? You got to learn to appreciate our handiwork," Hamer scoffed at Todd.

"I do, sir, but I done most of the work and I am tired,"

Todd getting back on his horse.

"You are going to report this now. You will say that they were bandits fighting bandits and they got what they deserved. You will be the first officer on the scene," Hamer said.

"Yes, sir," Todd responded ready to step up.

"This is only the beginning Todd. With that greaser plan coming out, now we will have carte blanche to do what really needs to be done," Hamer said taking a puff.

"And what is that, sir?" Todd asked.

"The end of the Mexicans here. The beginning of White Rule. Like it should be," Hamer said. Hamer pulled his horse to trot away. "I will take the other boys back to the station. Stay here a while then you go back and tell everyone what you found here."

Todd nodded and watched as Hamer rode away in the fading night sky. Then he turned and rode back to town. It was his best work so far.

In the distance he heard drums and the sounds of marching. "They are here. God damn. The army is here."

Unopened eyes no consequence
The door's been closed since he's walked in
The fight's been raging so many days
He'll greet you with a cross and a sickle
As he helps you in...

Tal'dos had been keeping an eye on that preacher since he saw him trying to stop a lynch mob. He was with Naomi, which only complicated the situation, but he couldn't help the feeling that he was somehow connected to all of this. The man never did anything suspicious though. He went around on his preacher duties. That was all. Tal'dos sighed and looked back through his binoculars. He had stationed himself on the roof of the building across from the church.

"Tal'dos? What are you doing?" Naomi's voice came from behind him. He had let himself be seen so he could get a word with her.

"I am watching your boyfriend," Tal'dos answered getting up from his prone position to look at Naomi.

"Why, may I ask, are you doing that?" Naomi asked putting her hands on her hips.

"Because Naomi, there is something not right about him. I can't see his past or his future," Tal'dos said.

"Tal'dos, I think you haven't found Chonnie yet and you feel helpless, so you looking for trouble where no trouble is," Naomi said.

"It has been months and still no Chonnie. I mean, he's just gone, and I can't see him," Tal'dos said it for the first time out loud.

"I hear you. I do. But Jacob is a good man. He's done nothing but good for the community. You got to focus your energies elsewhere. I mean, what about Bennie?" Naomi said approaching Tal'dos.

"Mayako is detoxing him. It's taking so long," Tal'dos said impatient.

"I thought you Indians were strong, patient, and

135

mysteriously wise," Naomi said sarcastically.

"The white man killed all those Indians. Now it's only us impatient and trigger happy Indians left," Tal'dos said playing along.

They both shared a chuckle together.

"See, I made you laugh. It will be okay," Naomi said trying to reassure him.

"Maybe I should meet him," Tal'dos suggested.

"Who? Jacob? I don't know," Naomi said unsure.

"It might be the only way to put my mind at ease," Tal'dos said.

Naomi thought about it for a second and then said, "Okay, but not like this. In your Rinche outfit. You will have to go as Talla."

"It's been so long," Tal'dos said dreading the tight dress and heels.

"Talla or no dice. Your choice," Naomi said.

Tal'dos grunted and said, "Alright. Tonight."

"Tonight," Naomi smiled.

The drums filled the air, and the sound of marching could be heard. Tal'dos and Naomi both walked toward the edge of the roof. They saw the military marching down Elizabeth Street.

You fall in waste
An open fire
You've got no taste for his desire
He brings you in to warm your bones
He's the reason why you came
And the reason why you ought to go…

Itsuko had spent many a night in an empty house. Both of her girls were grown and living their own lives. She felt so useless, but at least she still had Naomi. They talked like mother and daughter, but it wasn't the same. Junko was so angry at her about her father, and Mayako was off being a journalist and learning to be Kampo. They hadn't had dinner with her for months now. Chonnie was gone, shot by his own son, and Inez, pregnant and alone. It was the worst she had seen since those last days in Japan, but Itsuko rose from her bed as the sun peeked out over the ocean. She prepared to get ready to go back to the market.

"There was nothing as beautiful as watching you rise in the morning," Atoy said from her doorway.

Itsuko froze. She had not heard that voice since he died in her arms. "Who are you?"

"Itsuko, you know who I am," Atoy said walking into her house.

"No, Atoy is dead. He died in my arms," Itsuko said grabbing a knife and turning to face him.

"My love, you won't need that. I am not going to hurt you," Atoy said not moving from her blade.

"Why are you here? Why now?" Itsuko demanded.

"I'm not here for you. I'm here…"

"…For me," Hiro said appearing from behind Atoy.

"What is going on?" Itsuko said confused by all of this.

"You shouldn't be here, Hiro. Not yet," Atoy said annoyed at Hiro.

"I will not let you manipulate my sister. This is about me

137

and me alone," Hiro said.

"That is where you are wrong, Hiro. This is about all of you," Atoy said still looking at Itsuko. "Still as beautiful as ever."

"Get out! I don't know who you are, but you are not my Atoy," Itsuko said sticking the tip of the blade into his throat, but no blood came out.

"Itsuko, Hiro here, made a deal with the Shadow Lords and now is his time. The bill is due," Atoy said smiling.

"What deal? What is he talking about Hiro?" Itsuko said feeling dread overtaking her.

"All those years ago when the Shadow Wolf took you. Chonnie fought her in the shadows. Chonnie should have been banned from the shadows," Hiro said sounding defeated.

"But the hero here traded his life for Chonnie's ability to shadow walk. He had ten years and time is up," Atoy said and then swirling around, drove a blade deep into Hiro's gut.

All that Junko could hear was the scream of her mother. Junko jumped from bed and quickly grabbed her Escrima sticks and ran barefoot to her mother's home.

She arrived to see her father standing over the bloodied body of her uncle. Junko felt a rage that overtook her and charged at Atoy. Atoy easily knocked her aside and said, "The devil has had his due. Now, you are your friends are next." And then he vanished.

WAKE UP!

"It's always the most difficult thing in the world to face the fact that the world will spin on without you," Bass said chewing on a piece of straw.

The world slowly came into focus. It was a wide-open field. Golden brown wheat as far as the eye could see. A cool wind blew in from the east. It was the best Chonnie had felt in years. "This is the best. Isn't it, Bass?"

"Yes, sir. This is what we all fought for all them years. The West conquering us more than us conquering it. There's something about the West rolling through these towns preserved like a giftshop postcard, I feel the slowness of time. The bustle of a town on the brink of decay, like a dime store novel. The only constant is the single Mexican restaurant where all the trucks gather," Bass continued.

"There is also a calm to this place. No more fighting. No more atrocities. Just you and me sitting here enjoying the wind," Chonnie said feeling the contentment.

"*Movements come and movements go. Leaders speak, movements* cease. When their heads are flown. 'Cause all these punks got bullets in their heads. Departments of police (what?) the judges (what?) the feds," Bass rapped.

"Bass, what are you singing?" Chonnie said feeling a deep sense of concern.

"He can't hear you," Hiro said appearing from the horizon.

"Hiro, what are you doing here?" Chonnie said.

"It's time to get back in the fight," Hiro said walking without a limp and looking twenty years younger.

"What fight? That's all over. It's just this now, forever," Chonnie said looking back out toward the fields of wheat.

"Ahhh, Chonnie, you have no idea how important you are. Tal'dos, Junko, Mayako, Inez," Hiro paused on her name, "they are all still fighting for a better world. And besides your little girl is going to need you. Your fight is not over. Not yet."

Chonnie looked back at Hiro, "My little girl?"

"She is almost here. She will be special. Like some space princess general whose world has been destroyed. She will need you to help her through these dark times," Hiro said.

"But I can't stop it. The murders. The lynchings. The violence. Everything I do just gets me shot by my own son," Chonnie said feeling self-pity.

"So, you are just going to give up? Stay here with Bass for eternity?" Hiro asked.

"I have fought for ten years, and things have just gotten worse. What good has El Rinche really done?" Chonnie said looking at Hiro.

"El Rinche is hope to the people. What have you done? Look," Hiro said pointing at the horizon.

Chonnie was transported to a church where a little boy was strumming a guitar. He was singing.

No hace mucho tiempo
No sé la hora ni la fecha
Fue cuando los mexicoamericanos balanceaban en el viento
Y los asesinos portaban una pistola.
Allá en el Rancho la Plata
Nació el Rinche fantasma
Y toda la gente canta el corrido
Del fantasma que peleó con los rinches y él salió vivo
Todos menos la historia,
saben que los rinches son cobardes,
Matan por la espalda y sin misericordia
Para sus tierras robarles.
Tengan presente señores lo que hoy les voy a cantar,
De un Rinche Chicano que los cobardes no han podido matar
De nombre Chonnie de apellido Plata.
Dejado por muerto pero se levantó como el Rinche Fantasma.
Un par de ojazos con la mirada fría,
Tan verdes como la envidia.
Piel blanca, pelo rubio,
Y el pecho lleno de rabia y de orgullo.
Mataron a su padre Daniel
Su hermano Macario también.

Los Rinches que son cobardes
Cometieron ofensas que son imperdonables.
Todos menos la historia,
saben que los rinches son cobardes,
Matan por la espalda y sin misericordia
Para sus tierras robarles.
Se los tragaron a balazos
El plomo cayó a cubetazos.
La sangre corrió por donde quiera.
Y todo por un puño de tierra.
Dado por muerto, Chonnie fue encontrado
Y curado con cuidado Chonnie sanó.

"What is this?" Chonnie asked.

"This is what you have created. Your story is inspiration to those that have nothing but despair and terror. It is hope," Hiro said.

"What hope? I fail more than I succeed," Chonnie said.

"Let me tell you something, youngblood," Bass appeared next to Hiro, "I arrested over fourteen hundred men. I brought some of the most notorious outlaws to justice with just my wits, and yet, when the time came, they pushed me to the back of the room. Tried everything they could to push me out of the Marshall's, and I went from being a feared and respected lawman to a nigger walking a beat in Paris, Texas. I suffered all the horrors of Jim Crow and the hatred of the white man, but I never gave up. Not once. Not even when I had to arrest my own son. I never gave up. I found

142

you and helped you build something that has those crackers on the run. If you can't see what impact you have had, you are not the man I thought you were."

Chonnie turned toward the boy who continued to sing the corrido about his life story. Chonnie turned back to his two mentors and realized something for the first time. "Wait, Hiro. How are you here?" Chonnie said feeling the truth coming.

"I did what I had to do to keep you in the fight," Hiro said looking stoic.

"What did you do?" Chonnie asked as a shock threw him back into the pews. "Oww!"

"Hit him again," he heard Ginnie's voice say.

"I don't think that's a good idea," a strange, accented man said.

"Just do it," Ginnie said forcibly.

Chonnie was about to say something when he felt his body fill with electricity.

Ginnie stood over Chonnie's lifeless body with a couple of strangely shaped paddles in her hands. Tesla was engrossed by a large shelf of monitors and a large red switch.

Chonnie's eyes opened, and he said, "Owww. That hurt."

Ginnie laughed and said, "It worked."

"Thank God, another hit, and he might have caught on fire," Tesla said wiping his brow.

"Ginnie, what's going on?" Chonnie said trying to orientate himself to his surroundings. "Where am I?"

"You're at my ranch," Ginnie said putting the paddles back

on the table with all the monitors.

"You're ranch in San Diego?" Chonnie said feeling a wave of nausea overcome him. He turned and threw up on the side of the makeshift gurney.

"Careful there, cowboy. You have like a ton of drugs in your system from the surgery," Ginnie said.

"Surgery? What happened?" Chonnie said trying to remember anything past being in Inez's living room and Bennie coming downstairs.

"Well, that's what I want to know. You just showed up in my barn with two bullet holes. We almost lost you. Well, we did lose you but good ol' Nicky here made some equipment that helped bring you back from the land of the dead," Ginnie said laying Chonnie back down.

"I can tell you," Jovita said from behind them.

"Jovita? What happened?" Chonnie said confused.

Ginnie turned to see Jovita. "I told you to stay inside."

"I know, but Chonnie deserves the truth," Jovita said.

"What truth?" Chonnie asked desperate for answers.

Jovita walked over to him and said, "Your little bastard shot you and then you disappeared into the shadows. You have been MIA for six months and somehow you ended up here with Ginnie. Also, the Revolution is kicking into high gear. Did I leave anything out?" Jovita asked Ginnie.

"No, I think you covered everything," Ginnie said.

"Not everything," Tal'dos said from the doorway.

"You know for a secret hiding place, way too many people

know where it is," Tesla said to Ginnie.

"Don't I know it," Ginnie said wiping the sweat from her brow.

EL RINCHE

WHO'LL STOP THE RAIN

Inez looked out over the horizon from her bedroom window. A broken blinking light. Clouds sitting darkly on the breaking horizon. A thousand blackbirds perched on sagging palms. The wind breathed softly. This morning. Soft. Subtle. Not much to remember. But today. It is poetry. Like a teardrop. Nothing more than salt, water, & pain. She rubbed her round belly when she felt a kick.

"It will be any time now," said Señora García as she brought in her morning coffee.

"I can feel her kicking more and more every day," Inez said.

"It means she is growing impatient to be born," Señora García said with a smile. "Doña, there is someone here to see you," Señora García continued.

Inez stood up slowly and walked downstairs to see Mayako sitting in her favorite chair scribbling something in her notebook.

"Mayako, how good to see you," Inez said.

"Inez, oh my God, you are about to pop," Mayako said laying her notebook down and embracing Inez.

"I feel like it, trust me. How is Bennie?" Inez asked anxious for news about her son.

"He's doing well. He is at Kondo. His limpia is taking longer than expected. That was some strong magic," Mayako answered.

"Tell me what is going on?" Inez said gesturing Mayako to have a seat.

Mayako sat down and said, "Well, I have news."

"What kind of news?" Inez asked feeling anxious.

Just then Junko stormed into the house looking distraught and filled with rage. Mayako jumped to her feet. "Junko, what is wrong?"

Junko looked at Mayako and tears began to fill her eyes. Her lips began to quiver as she tried to get the words out, "It's… Hiro…he's…he's…dead."

Mayako felt her heart drop into her stomach. Inez slowly stood up and said, "What? What happened?"

Mayako knew the answer and said, "It was our father, wasn't it?"

Junko unable to speak, nodded, yes.

Mayako ran to Junko and embraced her. They both cried but Mayako managed to ask, "What about Mamá?"

Junko tried to clear her throat and said, "She's okay. She's preparing him."

"What are you going to do, Junko?" Mayako said feeling the rage boiling just under the skin of her grief.

Junko stayed silent a few seconds and then with a deep conviction said, "I am going to kill him."

MATANZA

Long as I remember
The rain been comin' down
Clouds of mystery pourin'
Confusion on the ground
Good men through the ages
Tryin' to find the sun
And I wonder
Still, I wonder
Who'll stop the rain…

EL RINCHE

WORKING CLASS HERO

As soon as you're born, they make you feel small
By giving you no time instead of it all
'Til the pain is so big you feel nothing at all
A working class hero is something to be
A working class hero is something to be...

"Hiro! Pay attention!"

"I am."

"Hiro, I know when a child is drifting off into space, now pay attention," said Hiro's schoolteacher. He sat in a room with ten other students from all over his village.

He was eight years old again. Feeling small and insignificant, he looked down at the notebook in front of him. He had drawn the great Hattori Hanzō fighting ninjas. Hiro was never as good at the schoolwork, or maybe he just didn't care enough. He wanted to be out there fighting with the other samurai. The ninja were everywhere, killing and creating havoc for the shogun.

When the class was over, Hiro packed his notebook and ran

out into the street. Today was the day. Hattori Hanzō was coming through their village. He was going to speak to the whole village. When he stepped out of the schoolhouse, he saw his sister with his mother carrying buckets of fish. Itsuko was not in class today because it was harvesting time, before the fish migrated up the sea. She was better at school them him, but she was too dutiful to stray into being a hero, like Hiro always wanted.

"Itsuko," Hiro cried out to her.

Itsuko turned and waved at him.

"Itsuko, come here," Hiro said waving her over.

She looked around. Her mother was distracted with Mrs. Nakato, so she ran over to Hiro. "What is it? Mother will not be happy with me shirking my duties."

"Hattori Hanzō will be here tonight. I need you to cover for me so I can go see him," Hiro plead with his sister.

"Hiro, I don't know. He's a samurai. I heard he's here to capture a ninja. You shouldn't be around that," Itsuko said.

"I know! I want to be there. Maybe he will make me an apprentice. Then I can go to that school," Hiro said.

"Oh Hiro, you can't be a samurai. We are not nobles. Only nobles can be samurai," Itsuko said trying to let him down easy.

Hiro grew angry, "Fine, I will sneak out on my own, and I will be a samurai. Just you wait and see." He ran off in a fit of anger.

Itsuko shrugged and went back to work.

They hurt you at home and they hit you at school
They hate you if you're clever and despise a fool

Till you're so crazy you can't follow their rules
Working Class Hero is something to be
Working Class Hero is something to be

Hiro slipped out when the family was readying for bed. Itsuko had come through and covered for him after all, although reluctantly. He made his way in the dark toward the center of town where Hattorio Hanzō was to speak. He was almost there when he saw something that caught his eye. It was two samurai questioning Mr. Nakato. He was bloodied and pleading with the samurai.

Hiro ducked behind a barrel of fish and watched. They were looking for Fūma Kotarō. One of the samurai pulled a knife and cut him across the chest. Mr. Nakato screamed in pain. Hiro couldn't believe what he was seeing. These were supposed to be the good guys and here they were torturing poor Mr. Nakato. He was nothing more than a barrel maker. Then he saw Hattori Hanzō walk up. Now, he will fix this, Hiro thought.

"Dear man, I know you are just a cooper. Making barrels for fish, but we are looking for a dangerous man. These men get a little over excited. Please, stand," Hanzō said offering his hand.

Mr. Nakato took his hand and stood on his feet. "Please, I don't know where Fūma Kotarō is. He is not here," Mr. Nakato said.

Hanzō laid his hands on his swords and said, "Cooper, I have spies in this village, and they have told me that you are the man who has been hiding Fūma Kotarō and his men."

"Sir, no I have done no such thing," Mr. Nakato said.

"Cooper, I have no patience left for you," Hanzō said as his sword sprang into his hand. He then sliced down from shoulder to heart. Mr. Nakato had no time to react. He simply fell to the ground.

Hiro couldn't help but gasp in horror and jump back knocking over a barrel. The three samurai pulled their weapons and turned to see a frightened Hiro standing there. Hanzō didn't say anything, he just nodded, and the two samurai approached him with their swords pointed at him. Hiro knew that they meant to kill him, but he was just frozen.

It was all a blur at first. A dark figure sprang out in front of Hiro. He then disarmed the two samurai and stabbed them through the heart with his blades. The two samurai fell to the ground, and he was face to face with Hattori Hanzō.

"Fūma Kotarō, now you die," Hanzō said gripping his katana with both hands.

"Not today, Hattori," Fūma Kotarō said and then grabbed Hiro and pulled him into the shadows for the first time.

Fūma Kotarō had saved him. A ninja. And he had seen his hero kill an innocent man right in front of him. It was too much to comprehend.

"Thank you, sir," Hiro said as they appeared in the forest.

"That man, Mr. Nakato was a good man. I was too late," Fūma Kotarō said as he pulled his mask from his face.

"I always thought ninja were the bad men," Hiro said.

"And the samurai were the heroes? I know. That is the legend they spellbind us with. The truth is that the samurai only serve the shogun and his nobles. Everyone else are only there to serve their needs," Fūma Kotarō said.

"So, the samurai are the villians?" Hiro asked.

"If it was only so simple," Fūma Kotarō said. "Let's just say that I fight for the people."

"A working-class hero?" Hiro said.

"Yes, I guess that's right," Fūma Kotarō said.

"Then I want to be a working-class hero like you," Hiro said turning his sadness to hope.

"It will be years of training," Fūma Kotarō said.

"I am ready to be a working-class hero," Hiro said standing to his feet with conviction.

There's room at the top I'm telling you still
but first you must learn how to smile as you kill
if you want to be like the folks on the hill
Working Class Hero is something to be

"Is that how it happened? I was so young," an old Hiro said, he was sitting in a rocking chair staring out on a field of wheat.

"Weren't we all," Bass said puffing on a cigar.

"Chonnie and Tal'dos and Junko are so young too," Hiro said.

"They haven't been young in years," Bass said.

"I have to go back. They need me," Hiro said.

"If only that were possible. They have to find their footing on their own. It is time for us ol' working-class heroes let the young ones be," Bass said.

"I hope I did right by them," Hiro said feeling regret.

"You did. You did. Now drink some of this sake with me. We have the future to usher in," Bass said raising the bottle to Hiro who smiled.

PART II

EL RINCHE

WAR PIGS

Generals gathered in their masses
Just like witches at black masses
Evil minds that plot destruction
Sorcerer of death's construction

In the fields, the bodies burning
As the war machine keeps turning
Death and hatred to mankind
Poisoning their brainwashed minds
Oh lord, yeah!

"I often try to understand why the world is filled with so much hate, so much blood," Mayako said as she stared down at the soldiers lining the streets.

"What are they looking for?" Bennie asked.

"They are looking for us," Mayako said as she rubbed her wampum beads between her fingers.

"They can't know it was us who stopped those rangers last

night," Bennie said standing up from the bed they shared last night.

"They are war pigs. They only know that they are hungry, and death and destruction is their food," Mayako said as she turned to Bennie who was gazing down at the soldiers on the street.

"What are we going to do?" Bennie asked her.

"We are going to do what we have always done. We are going to fight," Mayako said starting to get dressed.

"Are you serious? We are going to fight the U.S. Army?" Bennie said in disbelief.

"Not the Army. They are only a blunt weapon to control us. We are going to fight the fear," Mayako said.

"And how are we going to do that?" Bennie asked.

"We need to bring El Rinche back," Mayako said slipping on her shoes.

Bennie turned to look at her and said, "He's been missing for months. How are we going to do that?"

Mayako smiled and said, "You have his eyes."
Politicians hide themselves away

They only started the war
Why should they go out to fight?
They leave that role to the poor, yeah
Time will tell on their power minds

Making war just for fun
Treating people just like pawns in chess
Wait till their judgement day comes, yeah!

Captain William Street sat upon his trusted steed peering down on the open range. The vastness of the grasslands was as far as the eye could see. He had been given the post of watching the road from San Benito to Brownsville. This was the road where prisoners would never come back from. He hated his assignment, but he was a soldier, through and through.

"Sir, the Rangers are here," Lt. Red Quintan said.

Street lowered his binoculars and looked at the red faced, blond headed, West Point graduate, and said, "Very well, Lieutenant." Street pulled his horse down the hill toward the Ranger Captain.

"Captain Hamer, what can I do for you?" Street said through clenched teeth.

"Well, Street..." Hamer started to say.

"...Captain," Street interrupted him.

"Excuse me," Hamer said a little annoyed.

"Captain Street. That is my rank. Not Street. I am an officer in the United States Army," Street said asserting his authority.

Hamer gritted his teeth. He hated this Yankee, but he needed him, "Sorry, Captain Street. We are going to need your men to back us up. We got some bandidos cornered down the bend there."

"Are you sure they are bandits, Captain Hamer? Because last time..." Captain Street started to question Hamer.

"Of course, they are because I says they are. I do believe your orders are to help us secure the border. Direct from the President, if I ain't mistaken," Hamer said. He hated being questioned.

"Yes, Captain Hamer, we are here to secure the border

against the violence spilling over from the Mexican War, not frightened vaqueros with twenty-year-old pistols," Street said feeling like this was another massacre of innocent men.

"Listen here, Captain Street, I know you are new to this fight, but these are greasers. They are sympathetic to the Plan de San Diego. They want to take back Texas from the U.S. We can't tell who's a sympathizer or, God forbid, a soldier in this plot until we interrogate them. Now, your orders are to assist us, are they not?" Hamer said letting his anger be known.

"Yes, Captain, those are my orders," Street said feeling his own blood boiling.

"Then bring your men and let's get these greasers before they attack some upstanding White families," Hamer said pulling his horse away from Street. Not even waiting for his response.

"Lt. Quintan!" Street yelled.

"Yes, sir." Quintan responded knowing his Captain was angry at the entire situation.

"Bring the men up. We have some rinches to support," Street said as he pulled his horse away toward where his men were camped.

"Yes, sir," Quintan said as he hurried past his Captain toward the men.

> *Now in darkness, world stops turning*
> *Ashes where their bodies burning*
> *No more war pigs have the power*
> *Hand of God has struck the hour...*

It was more than a slaughter. It was a disgrace. Innocent men with no real weapons torn apart by Army rifles and powerful Colts. They stood no chance. Their only crime: Being Mexican. Street watched as these poor ranch hands were tortured. He knew these men weren't bandits. The Rangers didn't care. They had their own agenda, and it wasn't about securing the border from this supposed plot. For the past few months, Street had not seen any real evidence of any enemy insurgents, but what could he do, but follow orders.

"Hombre! Talk to me! I know you know where the sedicioses are. Just tell us and this will stop," Hamer said as he took a barbed wire bat across the man's back.

Captain Street closed his eyes and muttered under his breath, "What the hell?"

Lt. Quintan strode up next to Street and said, "Captain, we have to do something. These men don't know anything. These are just vaqueros heading home."

Street could barely make out that the man being tortured kept repeating something. "What is he saying Quintan?"

"What is that, sir?" Quintan asked.

"What does that man keep repeating?" Street asked.

"Oh, he is saying, 'Yo soy kineño.' Sir," Quintan said.

"What does that mean?" Street asked.

"It means that he is one of King's vaqueros. It means he is on our side," Quintan answered.

"Then why does Hamer keep beating him. It's obvious that man knows nothing," Street asked disgusted.

"It don't matter, Hamer doesn't make that distinction," Quintan said.

"In all my days as an officer in the United States Army, I have never seen such savagery. We are supposed to be protecting these people, not terrorizing them. We are supposed to be on their side," Street said wringing his hands. "Lieutenant, get the men ready to move. We are done here."

"Sir, Hamer ain't gonna like that," Quintan said.

"To hell with Hamer. We have done our charge. There is no danger here. Ready the men. We are returning to base."

"Yes, sir," Quintan said as he turned to leave.

Day of judgement, God is calling
On their knees, the war pigs crawling
Begging mercy for their sins
Satan laughing, spreads his wings
Oh lord, yeah!

KRYPTONITE

Well, I took a walk around the world to ease my troubled mind
I left my body lying somewhere in the sands of time
But I watched the world float to the dark side of the moon
I feel there's nothing I can do…

So many times, reaching the bottom of the bottle seems a futile exercise. That was what it was for Chonnie. It was August and he was still stuck at Ginnie's ranch…recuperating. The wound above his heart burned every time he lifted his arm. He now knew why Hiro drank so much.

"It's not so much the muscle pain. It's the pain in the heart that hurts the most," Hiro said.

He was sitting on the beach drinking his sake. It was his favorite spot. He would sit and watch the ocean lap up against the shore. And he would drink. Chonnie would often watch Hiro and never disturb him with his thoughts. He didn't know what pain really was until Bennie shot him in his mother's kitchen. Chonnie had fought so hard to stop an unstoppable wave of violence from the rinches. He fought his desire to take Inez and marry her. To show the world that he was still alive. The last son of the Plata's. He wanted so much to go back to his books and fight through the courts. It was a lost dream in a lost world. He was a ghost ranger now, fighting Texas Rangers with a mask and swords. It was all too much. And yet, every day he got up and went out there and fought. Then the bullet. The one bullet that he never saw coming ate him up. It sent him crashing into shadow. Only to wake to Ginnie and some crazy Serbian.

"Peso for your thoughts," Ginnie said blocking the sun from Chonnie's face.

"I don't think they are worth that much," Chonnie responded.

"You know that you aren't going to find answers at the bottom of that bottle of mezcal," Ginnie said.

"Maybe it's not answers I am looking for. Maybe it's the worm. Oh look, there it is," Chonnie said raising the bottle and seeing a bloated worm.

"I know you have been through a lot and finding out that Hiro is gone is a bad beat for sure, but…"

"But what," Chonnie cut her off, "I should pull myself by the bootstraps and keep fighting?"

"This war is far from over and we need you," Ginnie said.

"What's the point? Huh, Ginnie? Every time I stop them, they come back bigger and stronger. I am Sisyphus, cursed to push that rock up the hill every day only to have it roll back down and I start all over again," Chonnie shot his verbal assault at her.

"Look, Chonnie, you can sit here and feel sorry for yourself, drinking yourself silly, but there are real people that need your help. You are all that these people have," Ginnie said feeling anger simmering under her surface.

Chonnie stood up quickly feeling rage engulf him and stared Ginnie in the eyes, "I am no one's savior. I am a ghost. Not a spirit."

"You are more than a ghost. You are…"

"What am I? Huh, what am I?" Chonnie said putting his face a few centimeters from her face.

Ginnie could feel tears from behind her eyes begin to form. They weren't tears of fear or sadness. No, they were tears of despair. "Hope," was all she could say.

"Hope? How am I hope?" Chonnie said backing up from her.

"El Rinche is not some ghost. Some superhero fighting injustice. He is something more to a people who have nothing else. He is hope. You are hope…or at least you were," Ginnie said as she turned and walked away.

Chonnie looked up at the sun. He felt guilt overtake him, so he turned to stop Ginnie but she was already gone. "God damn it," he said as he took the last swig from the bottle. He felt the worm slide down his throat.

"You know, I have never seen such a disgrace of a ghost in my life," Jovita said from behind him.

"Jovita, not now. I'm not in the mood," Chonnie said throwing the bottle to the ground.

"No, we are doing this now. I am not Ginnie. I am not going to coddle your wounded, macho ego. I don't have time for that," Jovita scolded Chonnie.

Chonnie turned to look at her. She held a newspaper in her hand. "Jovi, what do you all want from me? I can't do it anymore. I was shot by my own son. I lost everyone. My family, Bass, Hiro."

"Jesucristo, you are such a baby. You think you are the only one that has lost people? You have always been such a drama queen," Jovita said taking a step toward him.

"Jovi, you always had great bedside manner," Chonnie said sarcastically to her.

"I don't do that because these are not times for self-pity. Too much is at stake," Jovita said.

"Are you going to tell me that the people need me because I am hope?" Chonnie said dismissing her.

"No. I am not. Because this isn't about you. You think you were the only that lost when the rinches killed your family? When Bennie disappeared? When Hiro was killed? No, Inez lost everything too, but worse, she lost you. The father of her children, and yet, she still gets up every morning and does what needs to be done. Now, I know that you have been dealt a bad hand, but that is no excuse for giving up," Jovita lectured him.

"Why not?" Chonnie shot back.

"Because if you don't pick that ghost up again someone else will and that person might not be as good as you at being El Rinche," Jovita said as she slammed the newspaper into Chonnie's chest and stormed off.

Chonnie grabbed the paper and read the headline: El Rinche is Back!

"What the?" Chonnie said as he unfolded the paper and began to read. "Oh, no!"

Chonnie started back to the house feeling his heart racing. When he approached the front door, he saw Jovita and Ginnie standing on the porch with Inez. She turned to see him.

Chonnie saw her face and her belly and said, "You are...so big."

Inez shot him her death stare and said, "We haven't seen each in six months and that is the first thing you say to me?"

Chonnie stumbled with his words, not knowing how to recover from his verbal blunder and said, "I..."

"Oh God," Jovita said, "still a mamón."

If I go crazy, then will you still call me Superman?
If I'm alive and well, will you be there and holding my hand?
I'll keep you by my side with my superhuman might
Kryptonite

EL RINCHE

SMOOTH CRIMINAL

Tal'dos hardly ever slipped back into Talla unless he was slipping into spy mode. It was his best disguise. An ambiguous Indian woman working as a criada for whoever needed it. The clothes never seemed to fit right, and the shoes were torture. But it was necessary to maintain his cover.

"Wow. You are really a smooth criminal, aren't you?" Naomi said to Tal'dos.

"There aren't many people that can sneak up on me," Tal'dos said in Talla's voice.

"A little trick I learned from a friend. What are you doing here?" Naomi asked as she began walking back to the seafood booth, she worked at with Itsuko. Tal'dos followed behind and said, "Something is brewing, and your boyfriend is involved somehow."

"Tal'dos, not this again. He's not involved in any of this mess," Naomi dismissed Tal'dos' concerns.

"Naomi, I have seen it. He is not the man you think he is. There is dark magic about him. I can smell it," Tal'dos said following her.

Naomi stopped in her tracks and turned to face Tal'dos. "Look," Naomi said, "I know you guys are having a tough time with Chonnie dea-"

"He's not dead," Tal'dos cut her off.

"Alright with Chonnie missing, but you have the army roaming the streets and the rinches are running out of control killing indiscriminately. I think Jacob should be the least of your worries," Naomi plead with Tal'dos.

"Naomi, I know it seems like I am grasping at straws, but I feel that he is involved in all of this somehow," Tal'dos said.

"Señora, señora!" came the frantic voice of a little boy.

Naomi turned to see Rodrigo looking scared. "Rodrigo. What's the matter?"

"It's the church. The rinches. They are..." Rodrigo couldn't say anymore.

"Let's go," Naomi said following Rodrigo through the crowded street.

Tal'dos had already slipped away into the shadows.

"Preacher! Come on out! We need to speak to you," Hamer shouted from his horse in front of Jacob's church.

Jacob stood behind the locked doors and sighed. This was the last thing he needed. Frank Hamer and his pet, Todd. He didn't know if they would recognize him from his past life, but he didn't have a choice. He was hiding three local vaqueros that ran from them after they saw Hamer and Todd torture and kill their friends. Jacob's church had become a refuge for la gente when they were being terrorized by the rinches. He was a known conductor in this Mexican underground railroad.

Jacob sighed and began to unlock the front door to confront the rinches when one of them said, "No padre! Nos matarán."

"It's okay. I will handle this," Jacob said with a comforting voice.

The man stayed behind the door when he opened it and prayed.

"Captain Hamer," Jacob said stepping out of his church, "how can I help you?"

"Preacher, I am hearing some disturbing stories that you are harboring some bandidos in your church," Hamer said leaning forward in his saddle.

"There are no bandidos here, but anyone is welcome to pray here. This is God's house," Jacob shot back at Hamer.

"Don't make me do this, Preacher. Just give them up and we will be on our way. No need for me to use force here," Hamer threatened Jacob.

Jacob felt the old feelings of anger begin to twinge in his hands, but he had no guns to act on. "Captain, like I said before. There are no bandidos here, but you are welcome to come back for evening service tonight at seven."

"You know, preacher, I know you protecting those greasers. I know because you protected them back in East Texas," Todd spoke up. His hand on his pistol.

"I don't think you want to go there, boy," Jacob felt Pablo's voice rising from within.

"Don't call me, boy. I know you a nigger lover with your black girlfriend and we let that slide because we got bigger fish to fry, but now you protecting bandidos. That is something that we cannot let stand. You feel me?" Todd said asserting his authority.

Jacob glowered at him and said, "Like I said, there ain't any bandidos here. Just me and my staff."

"Then let us take a look around and we will be on our way," Hamer said.

Jacob looked from Hamer to Todd and said, "Fine. Two minutes and then you leave and never come back."

Hamer and Todd dismounted their horses and pushed past Jacob. They entered the church and saw only empty pews and the Guerra's cleaning up. They searched high and low but found no one.

"Are you satisfied?" Jacob said from the front door.

Hamer walked up to Jacob upset by finding nothing and said, "I know you hiding them boys and I will find them. You better watch yourself."

Jacob just met his gaze and didn't back down. Hamer waved Todd to leave and so they did. Jacob had his hands clenched the entire time and let them relax. He turned and locked the door and then walked to the third pew and was about to press down on the trap door release when he heard the men talking. He couldn't hear it clearly, but he made out a few words…Norias…sediciosos'… attack…and revenge…

Jacob sighed and pressed the release lever. The pew slid back, and the men climbed out. "They're gone, but you better wait for nightfall to leave. They are probably watching us right now."

Naomi and Rodrigo rushed in from the back door and Naomi said, "What happened here?"

Jacob turned to her and said, "Hamer is on to us." Jacob helped the last of the men out of the hiding space and said, "Ve a buscar algo de comida." The men went to the back room where Mrs. Guerra was cooking up some lunch.

Jacob grabbed Naomi and took her to his office and closed the door.

Naomi confused said, "What's going on Jacob?"

"Those men are sediciosos. They were just talking about an attack on Norias. This is bad," Jacob said shaken.

"If they attack the King's, this is only going to get worse for everyone," Naomi said.

"I know, that's why we have to tell someone. We have to stop this," Jacob said feeling the itch in his hands for his guns.

"We will take care of it," Tal'dos said stepping from the shadows and speaking in Talla's voice.

Jacob, startled, said, "Who are you?"

Tal'dos smiled and said, "A friend."

"Are you going to need help? I mean you are a man down," Naomi said turning to Tal'dos.

"No, we got this covered. Just don't let on that you are onto those men, and I will take it from here," Tal'dos said and then disappeared back into the shadows.

All that Jacob saw was an Indian woman appear and disappear. "Naomi, you know that woman?"

"Yes, we are old friends."

"What are we going to do? We can't be harboring sediciosos, we are a safe haven. This could make it harder for those that really need help," Jacob said.

"Just stay the path. Steady. I have some experience with this," Naomi said walking up to Jacob and taking his face in her hands.

"You know I hate when you do that," Jacob said feeling himself calm down.

"I know," she said planting a kiss on his lips.

Tal'dos made his way back to their headquarters and was happy to be rid of the Talla disguise. He got back into his own skin and clothes. "What'd you find out?" Junko said from behind him.

"There's going to be an attack on the Norias Ranch," Tal'dos answered.

"The rinches?" Junko asked.

"No, worse, Aniceto and Luis," Tal'dos said turning to face Junko.

"What are we going to do?" Junko asked.

"What we do best." Tal'dos answered.

"He's not ready to go back out again. You remember what happened last time?" Junko said.

"I know, but we don't have a choice," Tal'dos said feeling the sadness overcome him.

"Yes, we do," Mayako said walking into the room.

"What do you mean?" Tal'dos said.

"Inez found him," Mayako said.

"Where?" Tal'dos asked.

"You wouldn't believe me if I told you," Mayako said slamming down a letter from Jovita.

Tal'dos and Junko looked down and saw the name, Virginia Yeager, San Diego, Texas.

BULLET WITH BUTTERFLY WINGS

The world is a vampire
Sent to drain
Secret destroyers
Hold you up to the flames
And what do I get
For my pain?
Betrayed desires
And a piece of the game…

"It all happened so fast. It always does. The moments that set the world on fire. This time it was a bullet with butterfly wings because it was destiny, they say. Destiny that brought that young man to the streets of Sarajevo. He hated us, you know. Called us dogs, vermin, pigs, thieves. He didn't know we were just people trying to live. He was taught to hate us, Bosnians. We were just the perfect target. Foreigners in our own lands ruled by a king who cared more for his pomp and extravagance than feeding his people," Tesla said as he took a drink of his whiskey.

"What do you mean, bullet with butterfly wings?" Chonnie asked.

Tesla laughed and said, "A miracle bullet. This young man was a nationalist, you see, and they say he had a chance to shoot him earlier that day, but he couldn't do it. So, he went to eat lunch. When he came out, there he was. The Archduke, waving to an adoring crowd. This was destiny and, in that moment, he knew it. So, he pulled his gun and shot him and his wife dead."

"I'm sorry about that," Chonnie said.

"Don't be. I wanted the bastard dead too. All of us Bosnians did, but that death is now brewing a war and I fear that war is going to roll over the earth. It is a sign that the world is changing. No more royalty. Just ask the Russians," Tesla said draining his glass.

"Nicky, I think you have had enough," Ginnie broke into their conversation.

"Not nearly enough. It is what is happening here. Hatred runs rampant, and you Chonnie boy, are Gavrilo Princip. The boy that had enough of hate. These rinches are just going to keep coming if you don't stand and show them that you have a bullet with butterfly wings, too. You can change things too," Tesla slammed down his empty glass.

"I don't mean to start a war. I never have. I just want to protect the people. I want to punish them for what they are doing. It's just that every time I take one of them out, two more sprout up in their stead. Now, the army," Chonnie said.

"Chonnie!" Inez shouted at him from clear across the house.

"Sorry, got to go," Chonnie said standing and waiting to face the music of Inez's wrath.

Chonnie walked to the parlor in Ginnie's front room where she was sitting with Jovita.

"Chonnie, you have to go back. You can't let Bennie play at being you," Inez said with anger simmering just below the surface.

"I had nothing to do with that. I've been out of commission since he shot me and then got lost in time and space in the shadows," Chonnie snapped back at Inez.

Inez narrowed her gaze, knowing that he was about to go into a pity party. "Chonnie, I came all this way because Mayako finally found you. Here. For a reason I can't understand…"

"It's because this is where the Plan was written. Where the revolution is being planned," Ginnie interrupted. "It's like destiny knew you needed to be here."

"I don't believe in destiny, despite what Nicky was just babbling about," Chonnie said.

"This is more than that," Inez said. "With the military there now, things have gotten much worse and Bennie, just isn't you. He will get himself killed."

Chonnie grimaced and turned away from Inez. He knew he had to become El Rinche again. He felt it the moment he saw Inez standing on that porch. "I don't know if I can anymore. Swords and smoke bombs are no match for the U.S. military."

"Perhaps I can help with that," Tesla said from the doorway.

"I have some inventions that will help you. Just give me a day and your swords and I will upgrade you."

Despite all my rage, I am still just a rat in a cage
Despite all my rage, I am still just a rat in a cage
Someone will say, "What is lost can never be saved"

Junko looked down at her hands. She had just beaten a rinche with blonde hair. She had not felt herself since Hiro was murdered right in front of her by her own father.

"You sure that's all you know?" Junko said wiping her hands of the blood from his face with her handkerchief.

"Yes," he said weakly, "we know they're coming. This raid of theirs will fail. We have made sure of that."

"And what about the Japanese man leading them?" Junko asked.

"He will be there. He is leading the trap," the bloodied rinche said.

"Good," Junko said grabbing her Escrima sticks.

"You're gonna let me go now?" the rinche asked sheepishly.

Junko turned and looked at him with hate in her eyes and said, "You are already gone."

"What?" was the only word he could get out before he felt his world go black.

"Junko!" Mayako yelled out to her.

Junko looked at Mayako who sat directly in front of her with candles and incense lit all around. "I know when the raid will be."

"And the rinche?" Mayako asked.

"He is fine. He didn't realize it was a dream," Junko said standing from her seated position.

"You might not think these dreamwalks hurt them, but they do," Mayako said worried about her sister. "I miss him, too."

"Don't Mayako. Just don't," Junko said feeling the anger and guilt rising inside of her.

"You will have to face your pain, sooner or later," Mayako said rising to face her sister.

"Once he's dead, then I will grieve," Junko said defiantly.

"That won't fill that hole inside of you," Mayako said.

"I don't care," Junko said storming off.

Mayako watched as her sister disappeared into the night.

"We going on another mission?" Bennie said walking up past Junko.

"Are you sure you are ready this time?" Mayako said concerned.

"Yes, I am. I got this," Bennie said confidently.

"Because last time you almost got Junko killed with your little stunt. You haven't mastered shadow walking yet," Mayako said.

Bennie leaned in and kissed her. "I got this."

"Uh huh. If you think you can change my mind with a kiss then you got another thing coming," Mayako said pulling back from him.

"I have been training all day. I will be ready," Bennie said.

"Maybe, but just in case, I am calling in backup," Mayako

said stepping back from him and turning to roll up her medicine kit.

"Backup? Who?" Bennie said concerned.

"Sista Fierce, she's a real bad ass," Mayako said smiling.

"Who's Sista Fierce?"

Now I'm naked
Nothing but an animal
But can you fake it
For just one more show?
And what do you want?
I wanna change
And what do you got!
When you feel the same?

DEMONS

The dreams they come with a soundtrack. For Jacob they are songs he never heard before. Loud and melodic. They fill his mind with the scene of him with no face and his gun in his hand. Pulling the trigger over and over again.

"No…no…" Jacob mutters in his sleep.

Naomi was awakened two or three times a night for months now. She could see him dealing with demons in his soul. They came at night when he was most vulnerable. Naomi knew he had a past. A past he never spoke of. She was fine with that because she had a past too. She never told him of the true extent of who her mother was. Who her father was. The burning of her town. She dropped bits and pieces here and there, but they kept secrets. It was where the demons hid. For Jacob, they seemed to hide deep in him. He struggled every day.

Jacob sat straight up and looked around. He wasn't at the prison, he wasn't in Jacob's barn, he was here in his bed.

"Jacob, you okay?" Naomi asked. Her concern woven into every syllable.

Jacob hesitated and then nodded, "Yes, I am fine. What time is it?"

"It's late. Go back to sleep," Naomi said sitting up and trying to caress his face.

Jacob pulled away and said, "No." He grabbed her hand and set it down. "I need a minute."

He got out of bed and headed to the kitchen where he poured himself some water and drank it down quickly.

"Jacob, I know we never talked about your past, but…" Naomi began but then trailed off.

"Naomi, I know you mean well, but I'm not ready for that. Not yet," Jacob said.

"Jacob…"

"…Please! I can't. Not right now," Jacob said, "I am going to the church. I can't sleep anymore."

Naomi felt a tear form in the corner of her eye. "You can't let the demons win. If you do, they will eat you alive."

Jacob struggled to put his clothes on and then grabbed ol' Jacob's razor from the dresser top and stuffed it in his pocket. "I already made my deal. The demons, they win in the end."

Naomi didn't know what that meant but didn't respond. She just watched him walk out of the house. She let the tears overtake her when she heard a knock on her window, startling her. She turned to see Tal'dos waving at her.

Naomi wiped the tears from her eyes and opened the window, "Tal'dos, what are you doing here so late?"

Tal'dos shrugged and said, "Sorry, I've been here a while,

but I didn't want to interrupt. That was one heavy conversation you were having."

"Demons, Tal'dos, demons. They haunt us all," Naomi said.

"I hear you Sista. We got our own demons to deal with. That's why I am here," Tal'dos said.

I wanna hide the truth
I wanna shelter you
But with the beast inside
There's nowhere we can hide
No matter what we breed
We still are made of greed
This is my kingdom come
This is my kingdom come…

"One little Mexican…two little Mexican…three little Mexican…" Todd said watching the streets at five in the morning. He and Lenny Blue had drawn the short straw and were on the graveyard shift.

"What you singin' over there?" Lenny said to Todd, pouring himself a cup of coffee.

"Just an old nursery rhyme," Todd responded.

"Ain't it Injuns?" Lenny said, turning back to the window and taking a sip of his coffee.

"Naah. We out hunting greasers, not Injuns. At least not today," Todd said turning to face Lenny.

Lenny Blue had just recently joined the Rangers. His uncle was Representative Trent Blue out of Duvall County. His uncle Trent was the only father figure he had in his life. His pop was killed in the last encounter with Geronimo. A fallen American hero, as his Uncle Trent always told him. Lenny had been raised by his Mamma and his Uncle Trent. He would always take care of them. Then one day Lenny took up with some rough and tumble cowboys and got himself in trouble with the law. Lenny and his buddies had followed this Mexican señorita and had their way with her. Her screams were all he could remember from that night. But the trouble was her father was the local sheriff. So, they were arrested and ready to be hanged when Uncle Trent came in and stopped it all. The other boys were sent to Huntsville, but Lenny he got a commission in the Texas Rangers. So, here he ended up. Working with this crazy Todd Mayfair and Captain Frank Hamer. Here they could do everything he did that night and more and it was all legal.

"Well, looky here," Todd said sounding giddy.

"What you got?" Lenny said leaning close to the window.

"It's that greaser family that helps that preacher. I bet they know about those sediciosos," Todd said.

"I don't know Todd, Captain Hamer told us just to watch and report back," Lenny said. He hated when Todd got like this. It meant he was about to do a bad thing.

"Get your guns, Lenny. We doing this," Todd said checking his bullets.

Justicio and Leticia were always up before dawn. They

opened the church for the morning service at 8 am. They often arrived early to cook up breakfast for those in need. Rodrigo was always hard to rouse in the morning and Leticia was tired of waking him, so she left him at home. Justicio unlocked the front door and set to turning the lights on, while Leticia started the stove and began mixed the migas and salsas.

"Well, well, if it ain't Señor and Señora Greaser cooking up some good Mexican food. Yum." Todd said with his gun in his hand. "Where are those sediciosos we know you hiding?"

"Señor, there is no one here except us," Justicio said raising his hands.

Leticia stood still frightened by the two rinches pointing guns at them.

"Now, we know you hiding them. I will give you until the count of ten to tell me where they at or I kill your wife," Todd said smiling and cocking his gun.

"Señor, por favor. I know nothing about those sediciosos," Justicio lied.

"One…two…three…" Todd slowly counted.

"Señor, my husband tells the truth. We know nothing. We just work for the church," Leticia plead.

"Four…five…six," Todd continued.

Lenny watched feeling that this was not going to end well. He swallowed hard and was about to say something when he heard the front door open.

"Todd, someone's coming," Lenny said.

Todd put his finger to his lips and mimicked a shush.

"Justicio, Leticia, you back there?" Jacob said as he walked into the backroom. He saw Justicio and Leticia looking like they were trying to act natural.

"Padre, we…" Justicio began, but was cut off by Todd jumping from behind the kitchen door.

"Well…if it ain't the white traitor hisself," Todd said.

Jacob turned to see Todd and another man pointing guns at him. "Todd, what are you doing here?"

"We came to look for those sediciosos you hiding," Todd said threateningly.

Jacob was not amused. "Todd, this ain't the first time I've had a gun in face. Now, I want you to leave before you do something we both regret."

Todd got a crazy look in his eye and said, "You ain't calling no shots here, Preach. I am."

Just then the sky cracked open. Jacob felt the bullets whizz by. They were louder than he remembered. Jacob turned to see blood spreading across Justicio and Leticia's chests. They fell to the floor.

"No…" Jacob said as he ran over to them. He dropped to his knees. He grabbed them in his arms, but he knew they were shot in the heart. They were gone instantly.

Todd walked up behind him and put the barrel of the gun to the back of his head. "Now, tell me what I want know, or you are next," Todd said.

Jacob felt anger rising up in him and he felt Pablo Honey rising up as well. Jacob laid Justicio and Leticia gently on the floor and stood up to face Todd.

"I made a deal, you know that?" Jacob said.

"What you going on about?" Todd said confused.

"I made a deal at the crossroads and for over three years I have kept that deal. I tried to be a good man. I built something good here. But like all small men. You meant to tear it down. Because I can't ever have peace. Not me. Not ever," Jacob said as he quickly grabbed the gun and pointed it at the second Rinche. Todd pulled the trigger without thinking and shot Lenny square between the eyes, but that wasn't the worst of it. Jacob had a razor and cut him across the throat. Todd let go of the gun and clasped his neck. He fell to the floor trying to stop the bleeding. Jacob took the gun and looked toward the front door. There was Ol' Scratch, laughing.

Don't wanna let you down
But I am hell-bound
Though this is all for you
Don't wanna hide the truth
No matter what we breed
We still are made of greed
This is my kingdom come
This is my kingdom come...

EL RINCHE

VIOLENT

Lt. Red Quintan loved nights like these. It was cool. No sun to burn his face. No sounds but the songs of cicadas. It was nights like this that reminded him of home. Back in San Francisco. Not too cold, not too hot, just right. But here, things were different. Even the ocean smelled different. Quintan took a sip of his nightly coffee. He looked out at the night. Nothing moving. He didn't expect any activity anyway. Here they were camped deep on the King's land. The Norias Ranch. The sediciosos' had never even gotten close to hitting the King's. The skirmishes with the so-called insurgents were few and far between, but here they were making a show of force. The United States had to show that they were doing something about the threat of insurgents in their own lands.

"Captain, ain't much to see out there," Albert Edmonds said to Quintan.

"Albert, I ain't a captain. Just a lieutenant. Captain Street is out at Sauz with Hamer," Quintan said setting down his coffee on the porch railing. He pulled a freshly rolled cigarette from his breast pocket and his lucky lighter. He lit his cigarette and wondered how this colored man became such a respected hand on this ranch. From what he had seen of these people, they didn't give Mexicans high positions, much less colored folk. But here he was, Albert Edmonds, a black man in charge of the ranch while the bosses are away.

"Sorry about that, sir. I assumed you was a captain," Albert responded as he stared out at the horizon.

"It's alright Albert, easy enough mistake," Quintan said taking a long drag from his cigarette.

Albert stared hard out in the incoming darkness. The sun was not quite down yet. The ground was still yellow from the last rays of the days, but he saw something on the horizon. "The Rangers be coming back."

Quintan looked out at the horizon and saw a group of shadowed men riding toward them. "That's funny. They ain't due back til tomorrow."

"Maybe they finished their business early?" Albert said.

Quintan felt the hairs rise on the back of his neck. "No, I don't think so."

"It's the insurgents. They are coming," came the voice of Atoy.

Quintan turned quickly to see the leader of the Black Hornets standing next to him in full combat gear. "Albert, get inside and call for help," Quintan said as he flicked his cigarette away and yelled back inside the house. "Sargent, get everyone to cover. We got trouble."

Quintan turned back to Atoy, but he was gone.

"I hate that guy," Quintan said rushing inside and grabbing his rifle.

They claim that I'm violent, just 'cause I refuse to be silent
These hypocrites are havin' fits, 'cause I'm not buyin' it
Defyin' it, envious because I will rebel against
Any oppressor, and this is known as self-defense...

Luis del Rey rode at the head of forty men. Each armed and ready for revenge. They had enough. They were going to strike at the heart of the beast. "¡Viva la Revolución!" He shouted as they descended on the ranch. The shots rang out and he could see several people running for cover. Soldiers readied their weapons and returned fire.

Aniceto Pizaña led the southern front. He sat at the head of thirty men. This was going to be a pincer maneuver, trapping the rinches and soldiers in the middle of a kill box. He knew that this was the first of many battles that they were going to have to fight. But this one here felt different. There were women and children here. Luis didn't tell him there would be. Bullets whizzed by him when he rode toward the main house. He saw the eyes of a Mexican woman who clenched a baby in her arms, so frightened. Aniceto felt a twinge of regret. He raised his pistol and fired at the man behind her and rode off.

Luis and five of his men were pinned down behind the corral when he saw an opening to run toward the servants' houses. He kicked open one of the houses and came face to face with El

Rinche. "What are you doing here?" Luis said.

El Rinche didn't say anything, but punched Luis square in the face. He fell backwards and fired off a shot. It missed El Rinche, but he heard the sound of a woman scream. They both turned to see a Mexican woman shot through the heart. El Rinche turned back to Luis and knocked him out cold. He ran out of the house and looked up at the sky. "How did Chonnie do this?"

"Do what?" Naomi said siding up next to him. Her back to the wall.

"He killed a woman. I wasn't fast enough," Bennie said feeling guilt rising in him.

"We have to keep moving, Bennie," Naomi said holding her trusty rifle.

"I don't know," Bennie began to break down.

Naomi grabbed Bennie by the collar and put her face in his, "Hey! We are in the middle of a fight. You can't wig out on me now. Get it together. Grieve later." She raised her rifle and fired hitting one of the sediciosos.

Bennie turned and nodded his head. He ran back out into the night with Naomi.

I told 'em fight back, attack on society
If this is violence, then violent's what I gotta be
If you investigate you'll find out where it's comin' from
Look through our history, America's the violent one…

Atoy cut down several men with his swords. They were no

match for him. He moved from shadow to shadow. "Amateurs," he muttered under his breath as he threw a young sedicioso to the ground.

"How about taking on a pro?" Junko slipped from the shadows. Her trusty eskrima sticks in her hands.

"Daughter, you shouldn't be here," Atoy said turning to face her.

"You killed Hiro. I am going to kill you," Junko said taking her fighting stance.

"Ah Junko, if only you could," Atoy said dropping his swords to his waist.

Junko opened a barrage of strikes across his body and head. It had no effect. He simply stood as still as a statue. She stepped back confused and reconsidered her approach. She launched another series of strikes, using all her might, but he just stood there.

"You can't defeat me, daughter. Your silly sticks will never break my magic," Atoy said as he grabbed one of her sticks and pushed her backward. He stepped forward and began his assault on her. Landing blow upon blow on her body. Breaking her protective vest and knocking her to the ground.

Atoy walked over to her and leaned over and said, "I will spare your life today, but if you come for me again, I will not be so gentle." He then stepped back into the shadows and disappeared.

Tal'dos ran from the darkness and dropped to his knees to hold Junko in his arms. "Junko! Please say something!" he plead.

Junko swore she could hear Tal'dos, but he sounded so far away. She looked up at him and felt the world go dark.

Tal'dos scooped her up in his arms and began to try to take her to safety when he came face to face with a soldier.

"Hold it right there," Lt. Quintan said as he leveled his sidearm at Tal'dos' face. "You coming with me."

Tal'dos thought about several scenarios to disarm him, but all of them would require dropping Junko, so he only stood there.

Quintan noticed he was no threat with the woman in his arms and so he said, "You are under arrest."

It flashed like lightning in the night. It came from behind Quintan. A glow and a sound of crackling that he had never heard. He turned to see another Rinche character holding lightning glowing swords. The Rinche character simply touched him on the arm with the blade. Quintan felt the electricity shoot through his body, and he fell down unconscious.

Tal'dos looked at the figure holding the lightning swords and said, "Chonnie?"

I show no mercy, they claim that I'm the lunatic
But when the shit gets thick, I'm the one you go and get
Don't look confused, the truth is so plain to see
Cause I'm the nigga that you sell-outs are ashamed to be...

VOODOO

I'm not the one who's so far away
When I feel the snakebite enter my veins
Never did I wanna be here again
And I don't remember why I came…

Jacob felt himself slipping away. His collar seemed to catch on fire and so he tore it off and threw it away. He turned and saw the dawning of the morning light. He knew that everything about him would be revealed. So, he ran. And ran. And ran. Until he reached his home. The home he shared with Naomi. The only woman that he ever loved. The only woman who ever loved him. She was not there. The lights were off, and the windows shuttered. Jacob breathed a sigh of relief and went inside.

"Ohhh Jacob boy, you have done it now," Ol' Scratch said sitting at his kitchen table and drinking from a cup. It was a strange cup. It was silver and ornate.

"Why are you here?" Jacob said already knowing the answer.

"You know why. You broke your deal, your ass is mine

now," Ol' Scratch laughed.

"No, you said, I had to pick up my guns. I haven't done that yet," Jacob said.

"You have always tried to find a way out of deals, haven't you, Pablo," Ol' Scratch said.

"I can't lose this. I can't," Jacob said desperately.

"It's too late. You lost it already. Not because you killed those two men, but because you enjoyed it," Ol' Scratch said.

"No, I didn't. I didn't," Jacob said feeling the lie fall flat on his lips.

"Come on, Pablo. You are a born killer. You hid from yourself all this time. Taking a dead man's name. Taking his life. Trying to be something you not."

Jacob looked at him and knew that he was right, but he couldn't accept it. "No, I have changed. I am not that man. Not anymore. I brought this church here, I did that."

"Who you trying to convince? Me or you? Pablo, I've known you all your life, or should I say, lives. You need to kill. It's just your nature. Now, you might ask yourself why you do it? Well, that's always been for you to decide," Ol' Scratch said pulling a rolled-up cigarette from his breast pocket and lighting it up with his finger.

Jacob watched Ol' Scratch for a few seconds and then shook his head and said, "No, Jacob showed me a better way."

"Yes, then you summoned me on those crossroads. You made a deal with a demon. Did Jacob want that too?" Ol' Scratch said.

"I...I...I only did that so that I could..."

"...Hide. I know. Everyone needs to hide from who they truly are."

"No...no...I did what I had to do back there. They were going to kill me. It was self-defense," Jacob tried to convince himself.

"Really, are you sure? There might have been another way, but once you saw your dearest friends gunned down, you gave into the rage. And you didn't just kill those men, you used ol' Jacob's razor," Ol' Scratch said standing up and stepping up to Jacob's face.

"It was the only thing I had."

"Are you sure? You had that rinches gun in your hand. You could have taken it and shot him, but no. You took that razor and slit his throat. You drew that blood. Why'd you do that? Why Pablo?"

"Because...because..."

"It's okay, you can say it. Admit it."

Jacob looked at him in the eyes and said, "Because I wanted to. I wanted to feel his fleshy throat burst open. I wanted him to suffer for what he did."

"There he is. The hell spawn I need," Ol' Scratch laughed.

"I...I..."

"It's okay. This was always the way it was gonna turn out," Ol' Scratch said stepping back.

Jacob closed his eyes and pictured Naomi. She was beautiful and good and everything he knew that he couldn't have. Not really. Then he felt it. The voodoo entered his veins. The cold comfort of feeling nothing. He opened his eyes. Everything was different. "I know what I need to do now."

"That's it, Pablo. Become what you were always meant to be."

"My name is not Pablo. It's not Jacob either," he said.

"Who are you then?" Ol' Scratch asked pulling a mask from his jacket pocket.

"I am Vengeance," he said taking the mask and putting it on.

Vengeance walked to the backyard and grabbed a shovel and began to dig. After a minute or so, he hit something metal. He threw the shovel aside and pulled out a tin case. He opened it to see his trusty dragoons and holster. He put them on and loaded the chambers. He turned and walked back into Jacob's house. He stopped in front of the mirror and saw an ever-shape shifting mask with eye, nose, and mouth slits like the luchadores' wear. He smiled for the first time in years and walked out of Jacob's life forever.

Demons dreaming
Breathe in, breathin'
I'm coming back again…

Rodrigo awoke to the rising sunrays. He jumped up quickly realizing he had overslept. "Oh no, Mamá's going to be mad."

Rodrigo quickly got dressed and grabbed his guitar and ran to the church. There were already people on the street. That meant that breakfast service was already well underway. He knew that he was going to have hell to pay. Rodrigo ran as fast as he could until he reached the front doors of the church. They were wide open, and several people were standing around. The air was thick with sorrow and fear. Rodrigo tried to push passed the people, but the crowd was too thick.

"What's going on?" Rodrigo asked the tall Indian who stood in the kitchen doorway.

Grant turned to see a little boy with a guitar strapped on his back. "You don't want to see this. It's not for children's eyes."

Rodrigo peeked past him, and his heart dropped, "Mamá, Papá," was all he could say.

Grant turned to see the little boy's face turn from horror to sorrow and said, "I'm sorry, son. Come with me."

Grant grabbed his shoulder and turned him to sit in an empty pew. "Where is Preacher Jacob?" was all Rodrigo could mutter.

"He doesn't seem to be here, but someone killed the two men that killed your folks. Maybe it was him," Grant said trying to comfort him. "What's your name?"

"Rodrigo." He answered without thinking.

"Rodrigo, is there anyone that you can stay with while we sort this out?" Grant asked him softly.

"No, it was just me and them," Rodrigo said feeling the weight of it beginning to hit.

"What about this preacher? Where can I find him?" Grant asked.

"Are you police?" Rodrigo asked.

"Not exactly. I used to be. My friend, Naomi Reeves asked

me to check on the church this morning. That's why I am here," Grant answered.

"Where is Naomi? She would know, she is his wife," Rodrigo answered.

"I will find her. Let me see if someone can watch you while I look," Grant said.

"No, I will go with you. Naomi and Jacob are the only people I have left," Rodrigo said.

Grant couldn't say no, so he said, "Sure. Let's go."

Grant took Rodrigo by the hand and led him through the front doors when they ran into a well-dressed man.

"What happened here?" the well-dressed man asked.

"Who are you?" Grant asked.

"I am J.T. Canales. I am the local legislature," J.T. said.

"I've heard of you, the fence-sitter," Grant said.

"The what?" J.T. said feeling insulted.

"This boy's parents are dead because you and people like you do nothing," Grant said.

"How dare you?" J.T. said feeling the anger rise in him.

"How dare you? People are dying every day at the hands of the rinches. And yet, you do nothing," Grant said walking away from him.

J.T. stood and looked as they loaded the bodies onto stretchers. Then someone said, "This rinche is still alive."

SOUL TO SQUEEZE

"Have you ever held a wounded bird in your hands? Do you carry it to safe ground? Do you mend its broken wings? Do you lock it in a cage and marvel at your kindness? Do you set it free and leave it to fend for itself? What do you do when a broken life is in your hands? Close your fist?" said a soft melodic voice.

"Who is that?" Junko said from the back of her mind.

"I am you."

"What? That doesn't make sense," Junko said confused.

"I am the You who you have forgotten. The little girl who once dreamed of a better world," said the voice.

"Wait. Where am I? Why can't I see anything?" Junko said feeling fear fill her.

"Because you haven't opened your eyes," said the voice.

"Why can't I open my eyes?" Junko asked.

"Because you don't want to."

"Yes, I do. I want to open them wide," Junko plead with the voice.

"Then open them," said the voice.

205

Junko tried and tried but the world was still dark. "Why can't I open them?"

"Because you don't want to see. You aren't ready," said the voice.

Junko felt panic overtake her, "I do. I really do."

Junko felt a finger slide across her cheek. It was soft and comforting. She reached her heavy hand to the hand on her face and felt her mother's hand. "Mamá?" she said and felt the heaviness of tears.

"Okaasan," her mother corrected her.

Junko chuckled and said, "Okaasan. I don't know how to open my eyes."

"I know, my dear Junko. I know. You aren't ready," Itsuko said softly.

"But I want to be ready. I want to fix it all. I want to…"

"…to avenge your uncle by killing what you think is your father, but he isn't your father. He is a demon that wears your father's face. Nothing more," Itsuko cut her off.

"Yes, I want to end him. I want to feel like myself again, but I can't. Can I?" Junko asked knowing the answer.

"No, there is no going back. None of us can. The past is the past. We can never return to it. No matter how much we wish it. We can only carry it with us, and we must choose what to do with it. Either let it weigh us down with regret and anger, or learn from it," Itsuko said.

"But it's so heavy," Junko said.

"I know. I know. When your father died, I carried it with

me for years. I was filled with so much rage. At him, at Hanzō, at the entire world, but you know who pulled from that pit of despair?"

"Who?"

"You and your sister. I saw the innocence in your faces. You were so untouched by the evils of my past. You simply saw the world, bright and wonderous. That wonder never failed to put a smile on my face. Never," Itsuko reassured her daughter.

"But Okaasan, I can't feel that anymore. It's gone. All I have is anger," Junko said feeling a dam about to break inside of her.

Itsuko took her daughter's heavy hand and began to hum and then sing, *"I got a bad disease. Out from my brain is where I bleed. Insanity it seems. Has got me by my soul to squeeze. With all the love from me. With all the dyin' trees, I scream. The angels in my dream, yeah. Had turned to demons of greed, that's mean…mmmm… Where I go, I just don't know. I got to, got to, gotta take it slow. When I find my peace of mind. I'm gonna give you some of my good time."*

Junko could feel the anger begin to fall away like a snake shedding its skin. She sang, *"Today love smiled on me. He took away my pain, said, 'Please! I'll let your ride be free. You gotta let it be, oh, yeah' Where I go, I just don't know. I got to, gotta, gotta take it slow. When I find my peace of mind. I'm gonna give ya some of my good time."*

Junko felt the dam break inside of her and the tears rush out with the ferocity of wild river. She let all the pain envelope her.

"That's it, Junko. That's it," came the voice of Hiro.

"Uncle," she muttered through the deep sobs.

"I know I left you without saying goodbye, I didn't have a choice," Hiro said.

"I couldn't save you," Junko said through tears.

"I know, Junko. I know, but that wasn't your fault," Hiro said trying to comfort her.

"Why? Why did you..." Junko said but stopped short of finishing.

"...let him kill me?" Hiro finished.

"Yes, why?"

"That was a debt that had to be paid for all of you to continue this work. To continue to fight for justice. To save lives. But most of all, so you could live," Hiro said.

"I don't understand," Junko said.

"I know you don't, but one day you will," Hiro reassured her.

"But how are we going to carry on without you? How do we continue when everything we do seems like we are just making things worse? The violence, the rinches, they only grow stronger," Junko said.

"I know that is what it seems like, but let me reassure you, you matter. The work you do matters. It is doing more good than you know. Evil always seems stronger, but it always loses in the end. Do you know why?" Hiro asked.

"No," Junko said.

"Because of hope. Hope is power. It is what sustains us through all the carnage. All the pain. It is hope for a better world that keeps us going. We persevere. Always. That is the one power that evil can never understand."

"But what if I have lost hope?" Junko asked.

"It's never lost, just temporarily abandoned."

"How do I feel it again?"

"Open your eyes," Hiro said.

"What?" Junko said confused.

"Just open your eyes and see," Hiro said.

Junko took a beat and then with a simple action…

"Everyone, she is waking up," came the voice of Tal'dos.

Junko opened her eyes and saw Tal'dos, her mother, Mayako, Chonnie, Naomi, and Bennie looking over her, and in that moment, she felt it, and smiled.

Where I go, I just don't know
I got to, got to, gotta take it slow
When I find my peace of mind
I'm gonna give you some of my good time…

EL RINCHE

LANDSLIDE

It was a cool morning, Inez cradled her hot tea, her rebozo around her shoulders. She looked out at the rising sun. It was a red kind of orange, a new day was dawning. She didn't know if it was a good day, or another day filled with pain. She just knew that Chonnie was back, and this baby inside of her was rumbling more than ever before.

"Today is the day, Señora," Mrs. García said from the doorway behind Inez.

"I know. I hope Naomi is okay, she knew them well," Inez answered.

"She needs time. Unfortunately, we don't have it," Tal'dos said.

"You know you have a bad habit of appearing out of nowhere," Inez said not even startled any more.

"It's a habit. Chonnie around?" Tal'dos asked.

Inez turned to look at him and panic set in. "I thought he was at Kondo with you."

"No, he was gone this morning," Tal'dos said feeling a

211

sickness in the pit of his stomach.

"Tal'dos, what do you think he is up to?" Inez said in a worried tone.

"I'm sure it's nothing," Tal'dos said trying to calm her.

"Señora," Mrs. García called to her.

Inez turned to face Mrs. García. She was holding a note in her hand. Inez took it and read it, but before she finished it, she felt a warm liquid run down between her legs. Inez dropped her tea and began to rub her stomach.

Tal'dos ran to her and began to sit her down on the porch rocking chair. "Are you okay?"

"It's time," Inez said.

"Time for what?" Tal'dos said.

"The baby, she is coming!" Inez said and squeezed Tal'dos' hand as the first contraction overtook her.

Naomi struggled to gain her bearings. She sat at her kitchen table with an undrunk cup of coffee in her hand. Jacob was nowhere to be found, the house was in disarray. Jacob's collar lay on the table solemn and silent. She could feel the tears welling up. She had been up all-night waiting for Jacob to come home, but he never did.

"Miss Naomi," Rodrigo's timid voice broke the silence.

Naomi turned to the front door to see Grant Johnson and Rodrigo standing there. Naomi couldn't help it anymore. "I'm so sorry, Rodrigo."

Rodrigo ran to her and hugged Naomi tight. Naomi

returned the hug and held him tight.

Grant waited a minute but had to press her, so he said, "Naomi, where is the preacher?"

"I don't know. He didn't come home last night. He left his collar here too," Naomi said breaking from Rodrigo's hug.

"We must find him before the rinches do. He killed the rinche that killed Rodrigo's—" Grant stopped and swallowed hard.

"He is a good man, Grant. He is," Naomi said trying to convince herself.

"He did what any of us would have done," Grant said trying to comfort her.

"It was Ol' Scratch. He finally collected his debt," Rodrigo said.

"What?" Naomi asked.

"When Jacob found us, we were going to be killed. But… Jacob…he set us free," Rodrigo took a beat and continued, "On the road back. We came on these crossroads, he made a deal. I saw it all. He wanted a good life, he wanted to be a better man."

"What are you saying Rodrigo?" Naomi said horrified.

"He sold his soul for a new name," Grant answered.

"Sí, señor. He did. He made his deal with the devil," Rodrigo sunk into a kitchen chair.

"So, if he broke his deal by killing those two rinches, what does that mean?" Naomi asked.

"It means that I am his and I will do his bidding. I am Vengeance," Vengeance appeared at the front door. Naomi and Grant went for hidden guns, but Vengeance already had his pistol pointed at them, hammer cocked.

Rodrigo looked at him. A villain with a villain mask. He was dressed in his black suit but the mask kept shifting. He swore it was a different face every moment.

"Jacob!" Naomi shouted.

"No, my dear, Jacob is dead," he said in a voice that was not Jacob's anymore. It wasn't Pablo Honey's either.

"That's too bad, I needed to talk to him," El Rinche said from behind him. He placed a black gloved hand on his shoulder and Vengeance shook from the electricity coursing through his body. He fell to the floor unconscious. "Nicky, your toys really work well," El Rinche said taking the gun from an unconscious Vengeance.

"I don't know why I have to accompany you on these little outings. I am no fighter, I am an inventor," Tesla said from behind El Rinche.

"Nicky, ol' boy. That's why you are here," Ginnie said pushing past Tesla.

"What is going on here?" Naomi said.

Ginnie came up to Naomi and said, "I am so sorry, Naomi, and you too, Rodrigo, but there is no time to grieve. Not yet. We have dragons to slay."

Inez let out a glass shattering scream and squeezed Tal'dos' hand so tight, he thought she broke some bones.

"Owww," was all he could muster.

"Tal'dos, you have to get Chonnie, he can't miss his

daughter's birth. You have to find him," Inez screamed.

Tal'dos was able to wriggle his hand from hers and said, "I will." Tal'dos turned to Mrs. García who was preparing Inez's bedroom for the birth. "How long before that kid comes?"

"I would say three hours tops," Mrs. García said.

Tal'dos' mind flashed a thousand images. He opened himself up to the universe and the thousands of potential moments that have yet to occur. Then he settled on one, he smiled and vanished.

Junko sat up for the first time, her ribs still sore. Itsuko brought her a bowl of miso soup. "Thank you, Okaasan."

Mayako, who was sitting at the planning table writing away, looked at Junko and her mother and said, "Mamá? Can I get some soup too?"

"No," Itsuko answered sharply.

"Why not?" Mayako asked hurt.

"Because you still call me Mamá," Itsuko said turning to walk away.

"Aeeiii, okay, Okaasan, can I have some soup, please?" Mayako plead with her mother.

Itsuko stopped and turned back to look at her daughter and said, "That's better, Mayako, but that was the last of the miso." And walked out.

Mayako pouted and turned back to her sister who was smiling as she slurped her soup.

"Mayako, where is Chonnie?" Tal'dos appeared startling her.

"¡Ay Dios! You have to stop doing that," Mayako said with

a start.

"Mayako, where is he?" Tal'dos repeated his question.

"How should I know? I'm not his keeper," Mayako said defiantly.

"He went to Naomi's," Junko said annoying her sister.

"Thank you," Tal'dos said and disappeared.

"Why'd you do that?" Mayako asked.

"Because Inez is in labor," Junko said.

Mayako stunned that she knew, said, "How do you know that?"

Junko smiled and said, "Hiro told me."

Vengeance awoke with the splash of cold water all over his face. His mask dripping with scummy mop water.

"Was that necessary?" he said as he spit out the soapy water.

"Who are you?" El Rinche asked setting the bucket down.

"I thought that was obvious. I am Vengeance," he said almost laughing.

"Who are you really? You're not Jacob Freeman," El Rinche asked.

"I have been so many people, I can't remember anymore," Vengeance said.

"Why are you here?" El Rinche asked.

"I'm here for the same reason you are," Vengeance said.

"And what is that?"

"I'm here to punish the wicked."

"Then why hold a gun to Naomi," Ginnie cut in.

"I wasn't here for her," Vengeance said.

Ginnie took a step closer to Vengeance. "Then who are you here for?"

"I am here for him," Vengeance said looking at El Rinche.

"Why me?" El Rinche said.

"I don't ask questions. When the boss gives me an order, I just follow it," Vengeance.

"Who's your boss?" El Rinche asked.

"It's the devil. He has his soul now," Grant stepped into the room where Vengeance was tied up.

"Not the devil. I'm not that important," Vengeance said.

"Who then? Why are you here?" El Rinche said angrily.

"It's too late. The train is a comin' and ain't nothing you can do to stop it," Vengeance said laughing.

"Enough of this," Ginnie said as she walked up to Vengeance and tried to peel the mask off, but it wouldn't come off. "It's stuck. It won't come off."

"It's demon magic. You can't take it off, you need a curandera for that," Grant said.

"I don't believe in demons," Ginnie said giving up on the mask.

"Well, you should, Viginia Yeager, because we believe in you," Vengeance said.

El Rinche pulled Ginnie back and she walked out of the room.

"That girl's got secrets. Wooeee, does she! And when you find out my dear Chonnie... it will shatter your little band of heroes here," Vengeance laughed.

"Everyone, give me the room," Naomi said.

Chonnie turned to look at her. She nodded and said, "Please, I need a few minutes with him alone."

Chonnie and the rest exited the room and Naomi pulled up a chair in front of Vengeance. "Jacob, I don't know what you did, but I know you did it for the right reasons. You had to kill those men."

"One man. The other one is still alive. He's first on my list," Vengeance said.

"What has happened to you?" Naomi asked.

"Jacob is dead. Only I exist now!" Vengeance said angrily.

Naomi laid her hand on his and said, "I know you are still there, I can feel you."

Vengeance felt a twinge of Jacob's old feelings for her, but instead of letting it overtake him, he shook his head and grabbed her hand. "No, you can't have him."

Naomi pulled away and saw the demon standing behind Jacob. "There you are, Ol' Scratch."

"It's not time for us, not yet. Too much work to be done," Ol' Scratch said and vanished, taking Vengeance with him.

Chonnie rushed back into the room. "What happened?"

Naomi took her face in her hands and said, "He's gone."

UNDER PRESSURE

Pressure pushing down on me
Pressing down on you no man ask for
Under pressure - that burns a building down
Splits a family in two
Puts people on streets
It's the terror of knowing
What this world is about...

When Tal'dos used the long eye, it was like seeing a thousand puzzle pieces with no picture on the cover of the box. Seeing the future wasn't the gift. These scenes always flooded his mind. The gift is being able to sift through them and make sense of it all. He had to reach Chonnie. He wasn't going to let him down. Not now. He didn't have a lot of joy in his life of a ghost ranger, but the birth of his child was one of those. Tal'dos was damned if he was going to let him miss it. He slipped out of the shadows to an empty house.

"What?" Tal'dos said to himself.

"They are gone. You are too late," Vengeance said as he

fired a shot.

Tal'dos dove out of the way, but he felt the bullet graze his vest. Before he landed on the ground, Tal'dos launched three shuriken at Vengeance. All three hit him in the chest but he didn't react, he just kept shooting.

Tal'dos pulled his sword from its hidden spot on his back. He used the shadows to come up right next to Vengeance. He was about to cut the gun from his hand when he felt a hand around his throat. Vengeance had him in his grasp. Tal'dos looked at his mask, which was constantly shifting faces. "What are you?"

"I am Vengeance," he responded. "Time to die."

Chonnie brought with him everyone, a distraught Naomi, a grieving kid, Ginnie, Tesla, and Grant Johnson. They were at a loss for words on the ride back. When they arrived at Kondo, Chonnie could smell the scent of sulfur. So, he drew his swords and said, "Stay here."

"Like hell," Ginnie said pulling a strange looking gun from her skirts.

Tesla saw her pull the zapper and said, "Ms. Yeagar, that hasn't been tested yet."

Ginnie pointed the zapper at a tree and fired. A blazing ball of light existed the barrel. It hit the tree squarely and created a blackened hole. "Works fine."

"You people can't ever just use regular guns," Naomi said as she pulled her own pistol from the small of her back. "Rodrigo, stay here."

The three of them approached the front of their hideout while Grant walked around the back. His own pistol in his hand, he smelt the sulfur stronger than ever from behind the building. He found a loose board and peered in to see a young Japanese girl mixing some strange concoction.

"It's okay, Chonnie, it's just me cooking up some healing medicine," Mayako shouted to the encroaching group.

Chonnie lowered his guns, "Everyone, stand down."

"It's smells horrible I know, but it works a treat," Bennie said helping her mash up some poultices.

Rodrigo had never been to a real superhero lair before. As he entered holding Naomi's hand, he saw the cool ninja weapons on the wall. He was in awe.

"Are we just letting anyone in here now?" Junko said, from her bed.

"Guys, we have a new problem," Chonnie said, as he hooked gazes with Bennie.

As Vengeance squeezed Tal'dos' neck, Tal'dos could feel unconscious beginning to overtake him. He couldn't let that happen, so he wrapped his legs around Vengeance's arm and spun around causing Vengeance to let go. Tal'dos gasped for breath for a few seconds, but knew this fight was far from over. He sprang up and landed several blows on Vengeance, knocking him back. Vengeance stumbled back into the kitchen counter.

"There's more where that came from. Whoever you are," Tal'dos said.

"Don't you recognize me? After all, I killed your mother," Vengeance said.

Tal'dos said confused, "Pablo, Honey?"

"Not anymore," Vengeance said rushing Tal'dos.

Vengeance landed several blows on Tal'dos and lifted him up and slammed him on the kitchen table.

"You know, Naomi is not going to be happy about that. That was her father's table," Tal'dos said springing up and countering with several blows of his own.

"Don't mention her name," came the voice of Ol' Scratch from behind him.

Tal'dos turned to look at Ol' Scratch. In that split second Vengeance knocked him out with an uppercut.

"This is way more complicated than we have ever faced. I mean, demons and now the U.S. Army, and the rinches even more emboldened. How are we going to fight this? We would need a whole army," Chonnie said sounding discouraged.

"Like we always have, with a plan. One crisis at a time," Mayako said.

"Where's Tal'dos?" Chonnie asked.

"I thought he was with you," Mayako said feeling a bit of panic.

"No, we never saw him," Ginnie said as she took a sniff of the poultice that Mayako was making. "Smells like peaches and rotting flesh."

"It's not supposed to smell like roses," Mayako shot back.

"What are we going to do? Isn't it usually Tal'dos that comes up with the plan?" Bennie interjected.

Chonnie looked at Bennie who had been quiet this whole time. His heart skipped a beat because they hadn't spoken since he returned from San Diego. "We all do," Chonnie said looking around at the room. "We do. It's not always Tal'dos with the plan. I have plans sometimes."

The room stayed quiet.

"Chonnie, you can't be here." Junko said entering the room with Itsuko.

"What do you mean? We are trying to figure out a plan," Chonnie said feeling insulted.

"No, you should be with Inez," Junko said.

"With Inez? Why?" Chonnie said.

"Didn't Tal'dos tell you?" Junko said.

"Tell me what?" Chonnie said sounding panicked.

It's the terror of knowing
What this world is about
Watching some good friends
Screaming let me out
Pray tomorrow - gets me higher
Pressure on people - people on streets
Chippin' around - kick my brains around the floor
There are the days it never rains but it pours...

"It's nice to finally meet a Long Eye. You have no idea how long I have been waiting to find one," Ol' Scratch said as Tal'dos slowly opened his eyes.

"The feeling is not mutual," Tal'dos said.

Tal'dos felt his face on fire. That last hit was like getting hit by a freight train. He slowly tried to sit up.

"Where did you get your power?" Ol' Scratch asked.

Tal'dos propped himself up on his elbows and said, "What do you want, demon?"

Ol' Scratch laughed and said, "It's that spirit that I admire most. What I want is your Long Eye."

Tal'dos tried to spring up and attack Ol' Scratch, but there seemed to be some sort of invisible barrier between the two of them. "What is this?"

"That is a devil's trap. They are usually used to trap demons, but in this case, I reversed the spell and now it traps you," Ol' Scratch said as he pulled an amulet from his pocket. "And now, you will give me what I want, or all your friends are dead."

Chonnie jumped from shadow to shadow trying desperately to reach Inez. He didn't even stop to ask where Tal'dos was and why he never reached them. That was a problem for the rest of the gang. Right then, only Inez mattered.

He jumped his last shadow as he approached the front gate when he heard the crackling of dirt and then he turned to see a fist envelope his face before the world turned black.

JUST BREATHE

A hot August day is more than most can stand, but deep in this border town it was more than heat. It was searing. Naomi stood in front a group of people that knew the Guerra's. She didn't know if she could do this; stand before Jacob's congregation and become what she was never meant to be—a preacher. She scanned the crowd hoping Jacob would appear, but she knew deep down he wasn't coming. Rodrigo sat in the front row wearing his only suit with a string tie and a large, brimmed hat too big for his little frame. His guitar laying across his lap. Sadly, it hadn't been played since his parents were murdered. He sat there solemn and waited for Naomi.

Naomi spoke up from behind the caskets. Her voice wavered at first, but she clenched Jacob's collar in her hand and began. "Today, I start the longest eulogy. It starts today and lasts a hundred years before their bodies even know they are dead. It starts today with the tears of children, it will continue for generations. Today, we put to rest these two people, but that is not the end. It will continue long after the dirt is poured on them. Long after the

225

grass covers their tombstones, long after they are but names etched in stone for tourists to wonder on their lives. They will live on. They must, or what is any of this for?"

Yes I understand
That every life must end
As we sit alone
I know someday we must go...

"Why does a demon as powerful as you need my power? Don't you have your own powers of seeing?" Tal'dos said.

"Enough of this," Ol' Scratch said angrily.

"What are you going to do? Take it? Both of us know that you can't just take it. I have to give it up willingly. I have to make a deal," Tal'dos smiled.

"That used to be true, but since you eliminated the Anciana, I am free. You see she was my jailor. She controlled my every move, but now, no one is watching," Ol' Scratch said pulling a vial from his pocket. "Vengeance!"

Tal'dos' thoughts shuffled in his head like a playlist on random, but he could see nothing past this moment. Vengeance walked up to him and held what looked like a compass in his hand. "What is that?" Tal'dos said.

Vengeance just smiled and opened it up and turned the dial inside. A few seconds later, Tal'dos felt his wrists and ankles begin to burn as red glowing shackles appeared. "Wait! Wait! I thought you wanted to make a deal for my power," Tal'dos said desperately.

"Your friends are going to die, nothing is going to change that. I was lying," Ol' Scratch said as he pulled the stopper from the vial.

Tal'dos felt the shackles pull him to the ground and pull him spread eagle. Vengeance leaned over him and said, "Open up."

Tal'dos clenched his jaw as tight as he could and shook his head.

"That's okay," Vengeance said as he punched Tal'dos in the kidney.

Tal'dos couldn't help it and felt his jaw loosen. Vengeance pried his jaw open as Ol' Scratch put the vial to his lips. The power slid from him. It felt like his heart had been pulled from his body, and then darkness.

"Friends, I stand here before you, not to bury Justicio and Leticia Guerra, but to praise them. Listen. Escúchenme. Can you hear their suffering in the wind? Sung by the chicharas in the grass. Memories woven into their DNA like hair color or silenced lips. Escúchenme. Can you hear their stories through the shrug of shoulders? Through the calluses on their fingers. Can you hear them singing?" Naomi continued.

Of all the times he had been knocked out, this one hurt the most. It wasn't because it hurt, which it did. It was because he never saw it coming. The punch, the men hiding behind the gate, he was too distracted. Chonnie felt the inside of his cheek with his tongue and felt the swell.

"You know there are easier ways to get my attention," Chonnie said.

"Yes, but would you have listened?" Aniceto said.

Chonnie scanned the room and saw Aniceto and Luis sitting across from him. Three men by the back wall and two by the door. "I might have. We will never know now, will we? You've ruined that, Ani," Chonnie goaded him.

"Chonnie, this is serious. I thought we wanted the same thing?" Aniceto shot back.

"We are on the same side. We don't want the same thing. There is a difference," Chonnie said.

"Why did you attack us at Norias?" Aniceto said.

"We didn't attack you. We stopped you from killing some innocent people," Chonnie said.

"There was no one innocent there," Aniceto said feeling his anger rising.

"Really? What about the criada? She wasn't a part of this. There are always innocents who get caught in the crossfire when you attack like that," Chonnie said defiantly.

"This is a war. If we don't fight dirty, we will lose," Luis broke in.

"Sure, but haven't too many of us died? We have to protect the people. Not count them as collateral damage," Chonnie shot back.

"How did you know about the raid?" Aniceto asked getting back on track.

"We have ears everywhere," Chonnie said.

"Who are the spies you have in my army?" Aniceto continued his interrogation.

"This isn't an army, Ani. This is desperation. You and your San Diego boys brought the military here. Your little Plan is just getting more of our gente killed. Don't you see that?" Chonnie said getting tired of the questioning.

"Chonnie, who are your spies? Tell me!" Aniceto said rising from his chair.

It came fast, a metallic disk slid across the floor with a pulsing light. Chonnie closed his eyes, he heard the pop. Everything exploded into a bright light, in seconds, all of them were unconscious on the ground and Chonnie slowly opened one eye.

"It's okay. They are all down," Bennie said from behind his El Rinche suit.

"That's my suit," Chonnie said as Bennie untied him.

"No, this is mine. Mayako made it for me," Bennie said helping him up.

"We have to talk," Chonnie said sheepishly.

"We do, but not now. Mamá needs us," Bennie smiled.

"How deep is the red when blood is turned to rust? How loud the cry of a gunshot? How long is the memory when the ghosts are forgotten? How long can the earth swallow us after we have become ash? How long must pasts sins live until our genes can finally forget? Our dead are never buried. Left in the blistering sun, rotting like only the discarded can. Those of us left behind are never able to wake. Never know the solace of a final goodbye, no roses on coffins. No pallbearers to lay us to rest. Just the ache of bearing witness," Naomi's voice filling the church.

Practiced on our sins
Never gonna let me win
Under everything
Just another human being
Yeah, I don't want to hurt
There's so much in this world
To make me bleed
Stay with me
You're all I see...

The sound of silence was never so loud. It was a loud thumping of nothingness. No future images, no jump cut to half-finished scenes. Just silence. Darkness, like a poisoned blanket.

"Tal'dos! Can you hear me?" came the voice of Junko.

"He's in a devil's trap," Mayako's voice flooded in as he slowly opened his eyes.

Junko smiled and said, "We got you, Mayako's gonna break you free."

Mayako sprinkled some water over his face and the burning shackles disappeared. Tal'dos freed his hands and sat up. "He took it."

"Took what?" Junko asked caressing his face.

"Ol' Scratch took my Long Eye. I can't see anymore," Tal'dos said feeling the emptiness within him.

Did I say that I need you?
Did I say that I want you?
Oh, if I didn't, I'm a fool you see
No one knows this more than me
As I come clean…

Inez pushed one more time. Mrs. García at her feet telling her to keep pushing. She didn't have the energy, she was drained from a long day of labor.

"I can't. I can't," was all Inez could say.

Then she felt a hand take hers and she turned to see Chonnie standing over her, "You got this. She's almost here," he said.

Inez smiled and pushed one last time. She felt the baby slide from her and laid back down.

Mrs. García grabbed her and quickly took the baby girl in her arms. "She is here. She is here."

The baby started to cry a few seconds later and both Inez and Chonnie smiled.

"What's her name?" Bennie asked from the back of the room.

Inez looked at Chonnie and said, "Her name is Leia. A leader and a…"

"…a rebel." Chonnie finished.

"Maybe in the meantime we can find solace in the blowing winds. Maybe in the meantime we can find comfort in the rhythm of the swaying flowers. Maybe music can be our constant companion," Naomi said looking at Rodrigo and his guitar. "Maybe in the meantime we can remember that the storm doesn't drown the roads. Not for long. Maybe in the meantime we can find a way forward. With new life to remember for us." Naomi finished and took a step back. She took a breath and knew what she had to do now.

SWEET CHILD OF MINE

She's got a smile that it seems to me
Reminds me of childhood memories
Where everything was as fresh as the bright blue sky
Now and then when I see her face
She takes me away to that special place
And if I stare too long, I'd probably break down and cry…

It was a calm evening, the sun was slowly kissing the horizon. Chonnie stood looking out of Inez's bedroom window. He cradled his new baby girl in his arms. She was so tiny, so fragile. Nothing else mattered.

"You have really taken to being a father," Inez said walking up behind him.

"She is everything I have ever wanted," Chonnie said.

"Everything?" Inez looked at him with narrow eyes.

"Well, you and Bennie too," Chonnie quickly recovered.

"Uh huh," Inez said taking Leia from him. "Let me put her to sleep. You have a talk you have to have." Inez gestured toward the window.

Chonnie looked out to see Bennie sitting on the corral post. If he didn't know any better, he could have sworn that he was looking at himself as a child. "I know."

Chonnie made his way down the stairs and out the front door. He had no idea what he was going to say to Bennie, but he knew that this had to happen.

"You know, your father used to push me into the corral when I was sitting there like you," Chonnie said to Bennie.

Bennie didn't turn to look at him. "But he wasn't my father, was he?"

Chonnie felt his heart pumping faster. "He might not have been your father, but he was your Papá. He raised you."

"You know I wanted so much to be him. He was so strong, he commanded respect. Just like grandpa, but you, I never knew you. They only talked about you as the bookworm. Not good to work in the rancho. That's why they sent you away," Bennie said.

"All of that is true. I was never one for being a vaquero like Macario. I would rather avoid that kind of work," Chonnie said.

"But now, you are this superhero? Fighting rinches, fighting demons," Bennie continued.

"I didn't choose this life. I would love nothing more than to be with your mother and practice law, but that was not in the stars for me," Chonnie tried to explain.

"You think you could be a normal father? Now you have a daughter. You can raise her like a real father," Bennie said angrily.

"Bennie, I didn't know you were my son," Chonnie tried to

defend himself.

"It doesn't matter," Bennie said jumping from the post.

"It does matter. If I would have known, I would have been here for you," Chonnie said.

"You know that night that they were all killed, ambushed by the rinches that left you alive? You know what I was doing? I was on a train playing with toys. Dreaming of fighting bad guys. The good guys always won when I played. That is the lie they tell you about this world. That good will always win. So, we will be good, but that didn't happen that night. That night I lost everyone. My father, mis abuelos, everyone, and you...you were a ghost before you donned that suit," Bennie let it all out.

Chonnie closed his eyes and transported himself back to the day that Bennie shot him. "You know that day you shot me. I was nervous. Your mother was so happy to have you home, but I knew things were not going to go well, but because of her, I tried. I wanted to make amends for not being there for you. But then... then you shot me," Chonnie said and opened his eyes.

Bennie was looking at him. His face about to break into tears. "I hated you. I hated you for taking my mother from me. I hated you for being my real father, for Serafina, for everything. I hated you."

"That demon had control of you. I know that," Chonnie interrupted.

"It wasn't the demon. That was all me, I chose to listen to that demon. She didn't have to convince me of anything. I was so angry. There you were, you had everything. You were the hero. You had my mother. And me? I had nothing but hate," Bennie said.

Chonnie didn't know what to say, so he let his deepest feelings slide out of him, "I lost everything too. I lost my brother, my parents, everything. I was left for dead. If it wasn't for Tal'dos and…Bass…I would have died that night. And I can't be with your mother. Not in the day, only like a sancho in the night because I am dead. Ascencion Plata is dead. Even if we ever win this fight. I can't ever go back to being him. I am now and forever a ghost."

Bennie had never considered Chonnie's side of things. He had been enveloped in hurt and hate for so long. He wanted to say something but couldn't. He turned away from Chonnie and said, "You remember that song that Abuela used to sing all the time?"

Chonnie smiled and began to sing, "*Somewhere over the rainbow. Way up high. And the dreams that you dream of. Once in a lullaby, oh…*"

Bennie continued the song, "*Somewhere over the rainbow. Bluebirds fly. And the dreams that you dream of. Dreams really do come true…*"

Both of them together continued the song, "*Someday I'll wish upon a star. Wake up where the clouds are far behind me. Where trouble melts like lemon drops. High above the chimney tops that's where you'll find me.*"

"Then what happened?" Mayako said, too excited to wait for the end.

Bennie leaned over her and kissed her. "I love your giddiness."

"Don't do that. You know I hate when you call me giddy,"

Mayako said annoyed.

"Mayako, we have to talk," Bennie said sounding serious.

Mayako felt her stomach begin to flutter. "No, no, no," she said as she stood from the bed they just shared. She pulled the blanket with her. "I don't want you to say it."

"We decided I should go back to school," Bennie said.

"Why?" Mayako said beginning to tear up.

"Because I am no superhero, you know that. I am not Chonnie," Bennie plead with her.

"But why do you have to go. You can stay here and study," Mayako said.

Bennie got up from the bed and lightly caressed her bare shoulders, "You know I have to go."

Mayako couldn't help it, the tears came flooding out. "I know."

Bennie pulled her to his chest and said, "This isn't the end of us. I will write you every day. I will visit as much as I can."

"And I can visit you when you can't come back here," Mayako said trying to see the bright side.

"Of course. I love you Mayako," Bennie said surprised the words spilled from his mouth.

Mayako smiled and said, "I know."

Whoa, oh, oh
Sweet child o' mine
Whoa, oh, oh, oh
Sweet love of mine

EL RINCHE

She's got eyes of the bluest skies
As if they thought of rain
I'd hate to look into those eyes and see an ounce of pain
Her hair reminds me of a warm safe place
Where as a child I'd hide
And pray for the thunder and the rain to quietly pass me by…

TIMES LIKE THESE

Ginnie had seen the gang down, but never defeated. Here they were, not saying anything, Tal'dos cradling Hiro's sake and sharing a cup with Tesla. Junko rearranging the hideout weapons. It was a sad sight, and she wasn't going to have it.

"What's going on here?" Jovita said entering the hideout with Mayako in tow.

"Well, we got Tal'dos over there pouty over his loss to Ol' Scratch. Junko over there trying to stay busy because she don't want to deal with the fact that the team is shattered. Then there is Chonnie off with his new baby girl. They have all given up, it seems," Ginnie said angrily.

"This fight is far from over," Mayako said taking the center of the room. "Tal'dos, we need you to come up with a plan. We can't let Atoy and Ol' Scratch win. They might have beaten us, but they haven't defeated us."

"He took my Long Eye, I can't see anything anymore," Tal'dos said sulking.

"Well, tough titties, Tal'dos. You just give up then? Was the

Long Eye the only thing that made you special?" Mayako asked.

Tal'dos didn't say anything but drank down a cup of sake.

"Fine." Mayako said, "I have a plan."

"What plan?" Junko said, stopping cleaning the hideout.

"Well, I have part of a plan. That's why I need all of you," Mayako said slamming her journal down on the table.

Jovita stood next to Mayako and said, "This isn't a fight we can finish with our fists and throwing stars. This is bigger than any one of us here. That is why Mayako and I have been thinking, we need to bring this to the public."

"And how do you plan to do that?" Tal'dos asked.

"We need to get J.T. involved," Jovita said.

"Ha…he's a politician. What can he do?" Tal'dos said.

"He can bring these atrocities to the world. He can bring charges against the rinches. He has the power to hold hearings, and those hearings are public," Jovita placed her fists on the table.

"What about the demons? What about stopping them?" Junko said.

Mayako broke in, "I have an idea, but I need you, Junko, and Tal'dos, and the rest of you to help me execute it."

"I am in," Naomi said from the doorway, "but Ol' Scratch is mine."

"He is mine too," Tal'dos said standing from his seated position. "He took something from me, and I want it back."

"He took Jacob from me, and I will get him back," Naomi said seething.

"What about Atoy? He's working with the rinches and his

hornets are too powerful," Junko asked.

"Junko, you and I, must face him," Mayako said.

"But there is one other thing," Chonnie said appearing from the shadows.

"What's that?" Mayako asked.

"The sediciosos are going to take down a train. We can't let that happen," Chonnie said.

"How do you know?" Tal'dos asked.

"Bennie, he stole this from Aniceto when he rescued me," Chonnie said slamming down a train map on the table with a date and markings written on it.

Tal'dos walked over to it followed by Tesla. "They are going to derail a train."

"They are going after the money, their revolution is broke. They can't survive without it," Chonnie said.

Mayako looked at Jovita and said what no one expected, "We have to let them."

Chonnie stunned by this looked at Mayako and said, "What was that?"

"We have to let them," Jovita repeated for Mayako. "This is the opportunity we need to show the world what is really going on down here."

"Besides, we have to take out the real villains, or we will suffer more violence from the rinches," Mayako said.

"This is crazy. We can't let them do this, we are heroes. We are sworn to protect the people," Chonnie said filling with anger.

Tal'dos took a step back from the map and a glinting badge

caught his eye. It was Basse's Marshall badge, he sighed and softly sang, *"It's times like these you learn to live again. It's times like these you give and give again. It's times like these you learn to love again. It's times like these time and time again."*

"What?" Chonnie asked not understanding.

"Remember when Basse gave you his badge? Remember what he said?" Tal'dos asked.

"Yeah, he said we have to take out the…" Chonnie stopped realizing what Tal'dos was getting to.

"We have to take out the demons first or it will just get worse," Tal'dos finished.

"We have been thinking too small. Jovita has it right. We can't win this thing with punches. We have to stop reacting and think about the real problem. This is bigger than us fighting some rinches out there. We have to think about the bigger picture," Tal'dos said feeling the fire in him grow again.

"So that means we don't stop an attack we know is coming?" Chonnie asked confused.

"Exactly, because that is not our fight. We have to deal with the demons. Not just Ol' Scratch and Atoy, but the disease that corrupts men's hearts. Apathy," Tal'dos said.

"We have to make the world care," Jovita said.

"Exactly! We have to let the sediciosos do their thing. We have to do what we do best," Tal'dos said.

"And what is that?" Junko asked.

"We have to bring the people hope," Chonnie answered.

"And how are we going to stop them. They are demons,"

Ginnie broke into the conversation.

"That's easy," Tal'dos said turning to Mayako, "we follow Mayako."

Mayako looked at Tal'dos and smiled.

SABOTAGE

I can't stand it, I know you planned it
I'm gonna set it straight, this Watergate
I can't stand rocking when I'm in here
'Cause your crystal ball ain't so crystal clear
So while you sit back and wonder why
I got this f**king thorn in my side
Oh my God, it's a mirage
I'm tellin' y'all, it's a sabotage…

"Captain Street, this is the best approach. Your men will do as I say," Atoy shouted at Captain Street.

"Listen, I know you were hired by the Texas governor, but we are the U.S. military, and I am tired of taking orders where innocents will be killed."

"Attack that village. It is where the enemy is based. I won't say it again," Atoy said.

"That's a simple fishing village. There is no evidence of sediciosos' there."

Atoy simply stood his ground. He thought for a second

and then pulled a dagger to cut Street's throat, but before the blade could find Street's throat, it was stopped by an eskrima stick. Atoy smiled and said, "Daughter."

"I'm not your daughter, demon," Junko said from behind her mask. She was dressed differently with a pair of darkened glasses wrapped around her face and a black suit.

Street didn't know what to do or who to attack so he simply took a step back and pulled his side arm. "What's going on here?"

"Sorry Captain, but this ain't your fight," Junko said as she dropped a disc on the floor and a large burst of light knocked him and his surrounding soldiers out.

Atoy annoyed by the blast said, "I warned you. Your little toys can't hurt me."

Junko took a step back and said, "That was for them." She then pressed a button on the side of her stick, and they lit up with blue lightning. "This is for you." Junko launched into a barrage of strikes which Atoy was not prepared for. They knocked him from his feet.

He felt pain. He hadn't felt pain in years. "What magic is this?" he said.

"It's science, bitch!" Junko replied.

***

"Marconi is a moron. He doesn't have one cell in his body to understand radio waves. He stole my design," Tesla ranted to Ginnie.

246

"Nicky, you can't just say that. I need proof to take him on in court," Ginnie said exasperated.

"This is my proof," Tesla picked up a tiny black circular object attached with an inch long stick at the end.

"What's that?" Junko interrupted. She had been helping Ginnie and Tesla modify their weapons all night.

"That is a radio communicator," Tesla answered. "Put it in your ear."

Junko looked at the little device in Tesla's hand and reluctantly took it. She placed it in her ears and heard a voice coming through it. "Naomi, Tal'dos, this is Chonnie. Can you hear me?"

Junko turned and looked around but saw no Chonnie. Tesla looked at her and said, "They are not here. They are back in town. You can communicate with them just by speaking, they will hear you."

Junko said, "Chonnie is that you?"

Chonnie confused said, "Junko, what are you doing on the line?"

"What kind of magic is this?" Junko asked confused.

"It's not magic, it's radio," Tesla answered, sounding appalled.

"What's going on?" Junko responded.

"We are already in place, you have to get to the military camp. Mayako is going to meet you there," Chonnie said.

"Tell him, he has to say, Over and Out," Tesla said.

Junko looked at him and said, "Weird science guy said you

247

have to say, Over and Out."

Chonnie sighed and said, "Over and Out."

"Now you say, Copy," Tesla insisted.

"Copy," Junko said.

***

Naomi brought the items that Mayako had told her to bring. Jacob's bible, his razor, and a piece of chalk to draw the summoning circle. She felt strange drawing this circle in the middle of her kitchen, but she had no choice. This was the only way to bring Ol' Scratch here. Chonnie was on the adjacent rooftop watching everything. Tal'dos waited in the shadows.

"Ol' Scratch," she called out to him. "I want to make a deal."

Naomi looked around and saw nothing for several seconds and then was about to speak when he appeared. "Well, well, well… if it isn't the girlfriend."

"I've come to make a deal for Jacob's soul," Naomi said clenching the razor tight in her hands.

"You know I know that this is a trap. If you really wanted to make a deal, we would be at the crossroads," Ol' Scratch said.

"If you know this is a trap, then why are you here?" Naomi said.

Ol' Scratch didn't answer.

"Oh because of this circle here, huh?" Naomi taunted him. "You see, I know that you ain't no devil. You are just a demon and you got rules you can't break."

"You think you got the upper hand here? Well, you don't. This circle might hold me, but it won't hold him," Ol' Scratch laughed as Vengeance bust in through the front door. He was about to grab Naomi by the throat, but Tal'dos grabbed his hand.

"Uh, uh, uh, not so fast, demon boy," Tal'dos said as he threw Vengeance back into the wall.

"There is blind boy," Ol' Scratch said. "You think I didn't see this coming? I got your sight boy."

"I know you got my sight, but what you don't have is a friend with a rifle," Tal' dos said.

A bullet ripped through the kitchen window and landed dead center in Ol' Scratch's chest. Ol' Scratch looked down and laughed and said, "I already saw that coming." But he felt something strange inside of him. He was weakening. "What did you do?"

Tal'dos faced off with Vengeance who seemed to be stumbling. "You see, the sight doesn't really show you the future, it shows you glimpses. You have to learn to read those images."

Vengeance lunged at Tal'dos and they began to fight. Blow for blow, Tal'dos held his own, but then Vengeance did something unexpected. He broke off from Tal'dos and came for Naomi.

Naomi stood there while he grabbed her by the throat and said, "One more step and she dies."

Tal'dos stopped. He weighed the situation. He knew he wasn't fast enough to reach Naomi. Another shot rang out hitting Vengeance in the back of the neck. He stumbled and let go of

Naomi. Tal'dos grabbed a dagger that was lit blue and was about to stab Vengeance when Naomi stepped in front of him. "Naomi, he has to be stopped," Tal'dos plead with her.

"No, Jacob is still in there. I know it," Naomi said as Vengeance rushed at Tal'dos and knocked the dagger from his hand. He began to squeeze Tal'do's neck. Tal'dos felt the life being choked from him. Another shot, but this time it didn't faze Vengeance as it entered his back.

Vengeance just continued to squeeze.

"Jacob," Naomi said in a calm voice Vengeance wasn't expecting. "Please, stop." Naomi stepped up next to Vengeance and showed him Jacob's collar. Vengeance couldn't help but let go of Tal'dos. He stepped back. "I know you are a good man. I don't care about this deal you made. I know you are still in there. I know because I love you."

Jacob could feel himself gaining control again. Vengeance was strong, but Jacob could feel a break in his control. "Naomi," Jacob's voice came back, "I can't stop this. I stole this life. This name. Everything. And I…" Jacob felt a stabbing pain in his heart. Like something clawing its way out.

"Jacob is gone," Ol' Scratch said. "He made the deal. There ain't no breaking those deals. He is mine."

Vengeance took back control and wiped a hole in the circle. Ol' Scratch smiled and snapped his fingers. Tal'dos, Naomi, and Chonnie felt the coldness strike their hearts. "You think I didn't see this? I have been around longer than you know. I have seen all of man's tricks. The arrogance to think that you could kill a demon. Many have tried and they have all failed," Ol' Scratch said twisting his fingers like turning a knob. The pain intensified for all three of them. Tal'dos fell to the floor, Chonnie couldn't hold the rifle anymore. He was laying twisted on the rooftop. Naomi was knocked to her knees, she could feel the darkness coming over her, but before she lost consciousness, she handed Vengeance Jacob's collar. Vengeance took it and clenched it in his fist. He turned to Ol' Scratch and took him in an embrace.

"You may be an immortal demon, but I am your Hell spawn," Vengeance said as he pointed his gun at Ol' Scratch's back shooting them both through the heart. Ol' Scratch pulled away from Vengeance's embrace and looked shocked. "No, it's not possible."

"We are both going to hell now, where we belong." Jacob emerged and fell back. Ol' Scratch felt his powers shrink from him. At that moment, Naomi threw a glass vial at Ol' Scratch's feet and it cracked open. It began to suck him into a black hole in the floor.

Ol' Scratch screamed and said, "No! I won't go. I won't!" He held his ground against the pull. Jacob saw this and with his last bit of strength, he stood up and pushed Ol' Scratch and himself into the abyss. In an instant they were both gone.

"NO!!! Jacob!" Naomi cried out, but it was too late. They were gone.

***

"Someone once told me, the world only makes sense when

you stop trying to force it to be what you want it to be," Junko said to a beaten and bloodied Atoy.

"You cannot kill me, Junko," Atoy said feeling his body failing him.

Mayako appeared from the shadows and said, "I know we can't kill you. We aren't trying to. We just needed to distract you."

"Mayako, you take after your grandmother, a witch," Atoy said.

"I'd rather be a witch, than a punk ass demon who can't even show his own face," Mayako said. "Ginnie, are we ready?"

"As ready as a 70-pound mirror can be," Ginnie said wheeling in a large ornate mirror.

"I found this mirror in Captain Street's quarters. He must be really vain, but it is exactly what I need. You see, like my witchy grandmother, I read. And what I read about you is that you really don't like mirrors because they reveal your true self, and demons like you hate that," Mayako said.

"What are you going to do?" Atoy said sounding scared for the first time.

"You are going back to where you belong. No more chaos for you," Junko said as she picked him up by his collar and dragged him to the mirror. "Now, look at yourself."

Junko grabbed his head and opened his eyelids. Atoy began to scream and to wither. His face changing to something unrecognizable. Mayako looked up at Junko and said, "Now."

Junko pulled him up to his feet and said, "This is for Hiro." And tossed him into the mirror which shattered. A blinding light encompassed the whole room and when they were able to see again, Atoy was gone.

"Is it done?" Ginnie asked from behind her own set of darkened glasses. "Is he dead?"

"Dead, no," Mayako said. "He's back in the spirit world. He can't cross over anymore."

All three women looked at each other and laughed. Then Ginnie said, "We should probably go. These soldiers are gonna wake up soon."

Junko and Mayako looked at each other and said, "Yeah, probably a good idea."

So, so, so, so listen up 'cause you can't say nothin'
You'll shut me down with a push of your button?
But you, I'm out and I'm gone
I'll tell you now, I keep it on and on

'Cause what you see you might not get
And we can bet, so don't you get souped yet
You're scheming on a thing that's a mirage
I'm trying to tell you now, it's sabotage...

EL RINCHE

DISARM

J.T. Canales was horrified by what he was reading in the paper.

On October 18, 1915, at about 10:00pm, around 60-100 Mexican bandits derailed and burned the Saint Louis, Brownsville and Mexico passenger train number 101 six and a half miles North of Brownsville. The bomb attack on the two-passenger car train occurred as it was on its way from Harlingen to Brownsville. Spikes and fish plates were removed from the track and then the bandits used a wire cable to pull the rail to one side just as the train approached.

He read the story in the Brownsville Herald, coffee in one hand. He set the coffee on his desk and sat down. He quickly looked up to see Jovita Idar sitting right in front of him. He jumped. "Jesus, how'd you get in here," he said.

"I have friends with skills," she responded.

"What do you want, Jovita?" J.T. asked taking a sip from his coffee.

"You ever heard the story of the creation of man? Oh, not

the Christian one, but one closer to home. You see, the Indians around here used to tell it all the time to their kids," Jovita Idar said.

"Is there a point to this?" J.T. Canales said not happy about this conversation.

"You see, the way the Indians tell it, the white man's God made the white man in his own image. He shaped them from clay and let them live happy lives. The problem was that after a while they had no ambition to do anything but eat and sleep, and they eventually just died off. Withered away like un-watered plants. So, he tried again. This time he poked a hole in their hearts. A hole that constantly needed to be filled. This seemed to work because that created want. Ambition if you will. First, they filled it with food and sex and the pleasures of the flesh, but that wasn't enough. So, they began to grow cities and states and kingdoms, but that wasn't enough. They began to kill and conquer and take from everyone else. They killed and they conquered so much that they began to destroy the world that God had created for them. This troubled their God, so he showed himself to them. A being of infinite love and cruelty. They then began to kill and conquer for him. Their creator. Until that didn't fill them anymore. So, you know what they did next?" Jovita said staring at J.T.

"What did they do?" J.T. asked.

"They came for him," Jovita said.

"Well, that's certainly an interesting story. But I don't see..." J.T. said trying get out of the conversation.

"That's the problem J.T. You don't see," Jovita smiled.

A bag went over J.T.'s head and then a zap that turned his whole world black.

I used to be a little boy
So old in my shoes
And what I choose is my choice
What's a boy supposed to do?
The killer in me is the killer in you, my love
I send this smile over to you…

"Well, this has been fun," Ginnie said as she packed her and Tesla's stuff into her car.

"I'm sorry you became part of all of this," Chonnie said holding his new baby girl.

Inez stood beside him, "Where will you go now?"

"First, I got to file that lawsuit for Nicky, then back to the ranch. Duvall County needs a good lawyer," Ginnie said and smiled. "You two, take care of that little girl. She is truly a miracle."

Tesla walked up to them and handed Inez a leather-bound journal. "For when she is old enough. She has the gift of science, I can see it in her eyes. Okay," he said and quickly turned around and left.

"What a strange little man," Inez said.

"He grows on ya'," Ginnie said as she gave Inez a hug.

Ginne walked to the car and looked back at Chonnie and Inez so happy with their new daughter. She pulled a locket from around her neck and opened to reveal a picture of a ten-year-old girl. She squeezed it tight and muttered under her breath, "They can never know about you, Lizzie."

"Who is that?" Tesla asked her.

"She's my daughter," Ginnie said as she jumped into the driver's seat and revved the engine.

"Is that secret something that they should know?" Tesla said.

"He isn't ready," Ginnie said slipping the car into gear and tearing off.

"Sake for your thoughts," Tal'dos said to Junko as she looked over Hiro's things.

"Hiro was more of a father to me than my own father ever was," Junko said.

"Are you ready?" Tal'dos asked as he picked up a simple black urn.

Junko, Mayako, Itsuko and Tal'dos walked out to the beach that Hiro loved. They stood there staring at the waves crash against the shore. "This was his favorite spot. He loved coming out here in the mornings and watch the sun rise," Junko said.

"He came out here to drink sake," Itsuko said.

"He did love his sake," Tal'dos said.

"I miss him," Mayako said feeling the tears travel down her face.

"We all do," Junko said as she opened the top of the urn and poured the ashes into the sea.

Tal'dos pulled four shot glasses out and handed them out to

each of them. He poured sake in each of their glasses. Tal'dos raised his glass and said, "Here's to you, you old drunk."

They all drank down the sake and then began to cough. "This stuff is terrible," Mayako finally said.

Itsuko was the only one who didn't cough. She poured herself another cup and said, "This is what we grew up drinking in Japan. Hiro made it here in the empty fish barrels."

Tal'dos looked horrified and said, "He made it in fish guts?"

Itsuko drank down the second glass and smiled, then walked away.

Naomi looked around her destroyed house. She didn't have the strength to clean up. She just felt lost. Then she heard a guitar strumming from outside. She walked out and saw Rodrigo beginning to play.

"He's not gone, you know," Rodrigo said.

"What?" Naomi said sitting down next to Rodrigo.

"He's not gone. He lives on in us, like my parents. We have to honor them," Rodrigo said.

Naomi looked at him. He seemed so wise for such a young soul. "Well, our church doesn't have a preacher anymore."

Rodrigo turned to her and said, "Sure we do." He never stopped strumming.

"Do you think they will accept me? A woman preacher?" Naomi asked.

"Why not? We had a cursed white Hell spawn preacher. A woman is just what we need," Rodrigo smiled.

Naomi laughed and turned to look out toward the street.

Captain Street had had enough of South Texas. From shady Japanese hired thugs trying to kill him, to magical ghost rangers, to the Rangers, he was ready to go home.

"The sediocosos hit a train last night. Should we go out there?" Quinlan asked.

"No, let the locals handle this. We are packing up," Street said.

"We got our orders to move out?" Quinlan asked sounding hopeful.

"I am giving the order," Street said.

"You shouldn't leave. Not just yet," came the voice of El Rinche.

Captain Street pulled his sidearm. Quinlan pulled his Ka-Bar. "What are you doing here? This isn't such a good idea, bandido," Street said.

"Captain, I am not your enemy and I have seen that you are not my enemy either. We both want the same thing," El Rinche said appearing from the shadows. His hands resting on his sheathed swords.

"Do we? I was brought here to stop people like you," Captain Street said.

"No, you were brought here to safeguard the people from the violence of a few. But you and I know that those few aren't the people you thought they were," El Rinche said.

"You talking about the Rangers?" Captain Street said

relaxing his gun.

"They are the real problem, but they are just a symptom. They are not the disease," El Rinche said.

"And what is the real disease?" Captain Street asked.

El Rinche threw down a copy of the newly minted La Crónica. The headline read: Texas Rangers Murder Hundreds to Steal Mexican Lands.

Captain Street looked up from the newspaper to say something, but El Rinche had vanished.

EL RINCHE

A HARD RAIN'S A-GONNA FALL

Oh, what did you see, my blue-eyed son?
Oh, what did you see, my darling young one?
I saw a newborn baby with wild wolves all around it
I saw a highway of diamonds with nobody on it
I saw a black branch with blood that kept drippin'
I saw a room full of men with their hammers a-bleedin'
I saw a white ladder all covered with water
I saw ten thousand talkers whose tongues were all broken
I saw guns and sharp swords in the hands of young children
And it's a hard, and it's a hard, it's a hard, it's a hard
And it's a hard rain's a-gonna fall

It was the constant clicking noise that kept Judge Stillwell awake. It was a dark night. That stars refusing to light brightly on this night. No breeze to cool. Just the click, click, clicking of the car's motor. Cucarachas they called them. These long black models that had quickly overtaken the dirt roads of these dusty South Texas Borderlands. They were the favorites of the Rinches. This year the violence that he had helped perpetuate had exploded. It was so out of control now that even Stillwell feared for his life on these long nightly treks from Brownsville to his home in Pharr. Sometimes it would take up to three hours to make the drive. He would often have to swerve around hotspots of violence. Rangers rounding up men, arrested. Some never seen or heard from again. He knew all about the San Benito Road. He had sentenced many "bandits" to jail and seen them whisked away by the Rangers down the San Benito Road. Their fate down that road was never his concern. Or so he thought.

It came from the ground. He was sure of it. Something jumped up and smashed into his engine. Causing the car to sputter to a halt. Bill, his driver, looked perplexed, but then a second later, he slumped down in his seat and was fast asleep. It was then that Stillwell realized that this was no rock that jumped up, it was something far more sinister.

He didn't hear it. He just felt it. The swift sting of a barb in his neck. Then all went quiet.

He awoke with a start. He didn't understand what was happening. His head was covered by a cloth. Everything was black. He felt the night air cool around his body. His coat was gone and so were his pants. He was sitting on dirt. He could feel that against his naked flesh.

"What's going on? What do you want?" Stillwell pleaded.

But there was no answer. Just the soft ticking of something in the distance.

"I will give you whatever you want," Stillwell continued to plead.

Once again, no response.

"For God's sake, say something!" Stillwell shouted out feeling the fear creeping down his spine.

Then it came. The voice he had dreaded for years. It was filled with anger and pain and vengeance. "For God's sake? Do you think He is even up there? Listening to your pleas? No, He doesn't care. He abandoned you here on the side of the road. He left you for me."

"What are you gonna do to me?" Stillwell asked.

"Why don't you ask your God? Maybe He will answer you. After all, you are a white man," the voice almost whispered.

"And what about you? Aren't you a white man too?"

"Let me tell you about you and your God. The good book gets it only half right. It leaves out the truth," the voice said with his low tone.

"What truth?" Stillwell said not liking where this was going.

"That there is a hole in the white man. Your white god put it there so that the white man will always crave," said the voice with a pregnant pause.

Stillwell couldn't stand the silence, so he asked, "Crave for what?"

"For everything. That's why it spread across the Earth like a sickness. It spread from place to place with his steel, his filth, and his need to fill that hole. They conquered and killed and burned everything to ash. Then they placed monuments to their successes made of stolen riches, stolen lives, and still, they could not fill that hole inside them. They turned to taking everyone else's joy. Their happiness was too much for the white man to bare. He had to have it. So, he took that too. And yet, the hole was still there. So, he took to enslaving peoples. Maybe crushing their souls would fill it, but it didn't. And he turned to massacring those that stood from them having everything. That hole led to so much progress and yet, the white man hungered for more. And when he gets the whole world, what then?"

"I...I don't know," Stillwell said feeling his legs begin to shake from the inevitable that was coming.

"Well, the white god didn't know either, so he tried to fill the white man's soul with peace and love and his own son, but when they killed him too, the white god began to lose all hope for his creation. A creation that was supposed to bring joy and love to the world but instead that hole corrupted everything. And one day, he realized, that when the white man has conquered and taken everything, that the white man will come for him too."

And with that, Stillwell felt the cloth pulled from his head and he saw that he was standing in front of a ditch filled with bodies. They were men shot and stabbed and thrown into this pit like refuse. Stillwell gagged at the sight of it all. The stench was worse than anything he could have imagined. He wondered why he couldn't smell it before. The bag must have blocked the smell. It was a hellscape. Stillwell could do nothing but look at the faces twisted from fear and the pain of their last moments. The ticking getting louder and louder. Then he felt the push.

"Welcome to La Matanza," the voice said before drifting away with the wind.

Stillwell fell on the bodies. He could feel the dirt and blood creeping onto his naked flesh. It felt like he was absorbing all of the horror through his pores. The ticking was now so loud, he knew he was close to the source, and then in the moonlight, he saw it. A shattered watch. It's broken hands still ticking away.

"Why did you do that?" said a nicely dressed Mexicano with a Texas twang in his voice.

"The time has passed for subtility, J.T.," said El Rinche with a voice so stone cold that it could only be filled with misery.

"This isn't you, El Rinche. This fight has corrupted you," J.T. said.

"I've tried to fight them one at a time. I've fought them for years. And yet, it has just gotten worse and worse. Besides, where have you been this whole time?" El Rinche shot back.

"I've been here trying to stop this, but they have the law on their hands," J.T. said.

"Then it's the time for outlaws."

"That can't be the way. Look at Stillwell, he is covered in all that blood and guts. Is that what you want? To see every white man lying dead in a ditch?" J.T. said with conviction.

"Tonight, wasn't for him," El Rinche said.

"Who was it for then?" J.T. asked but El Rinche had already

vanished.

And what did you hear, my blue-eyed son?
And what did you hear, my darling young one?
I heard the sound of a thunder, it roared out a warnin'
Heard the roar of a wave that could drown the whole world
Heard one hundred drummers whose hands were a-blazin'
Heard ten thousand whisperin' and nobody listenin'
Heard one person starve, I heard many people laughin'
Heard the song of a poet who died in the gutter
Heard the sound of a clown who cried in the alley
And it's a hard, and it's a hard, it's a hard, it's a hard
And it's a hard rain's a-gonna fall

Christopher Carmona is the author of *El Rinche: The Ghost Ranger of the Río Grande*, which was a finalist for the 2019 Best Young Adult Novel for the Texas Institute of Letters. His short story collection, *The Road to Llorona Park*, won the 2016 NACCS Tejas Best Fiction Award and was listed as one of the top 8 Latinx books in 2016 by NBC News. He has a chapter in *Reverberations of Racial Violence: Critical Reflections on the History of the Border,* discussing intergenerational trauma for Mexican Americans in the Río Grande Valley.